WHO COMES
WITH CANNONS?

BY PATRICIA BEATTY

Be Ever Hopeful, Hannalee
Behave Yourself, Bethany Brant
Charley Skedaddle
The Coach That Never Came
Eben Tyne, Powdermonkey
(coauthored with Phillip Robbins)
Eight Mules from Monterey
Jayhawker
Lupita Mañana
Sarah and Me and the Lady from the Sea
Turn Homeward, Hannalee

WHO COMES
WITH CANNONS?

Patricia Beatty

MORROW JUNIOR BOOKS
New York

10

Library of Congress Cataloging-in-Publication Data
Beatty, Patricia, 1922–1991
    Who comes with cannons / by Patricia Beatty. p. cm.
    Summary: In 1861 twelve-year-old Truth, a Quaker girl from
Indiana, is staying with relatives who run a North Carolina station
of the Underground Railroad, when her world is changed
by the beginning of the Civil War.
    ISBN 0-688-11028-2
    1. United States—History—Civil War, 1861–1865—Juvenile fiction.
[1. United States—History—Civil War, 1861–1865—Fiction.
2. Underground railroad—Fiction. 3. Quakers—Fiction.] I. Title.
PZ7.B380544Wh 1992 [Fic]—dc20   92-6317 CIP AC

CONTENTS

CHAPTER 1
Kettle Cousin · 1

CHAPTER 2
The Coffle · 12

CHAPTER 3
Station Six · 23

CHAPTER 4
Bad Neighbors · 38

CHAPTER 5
War Comes · 48

CHAPTER 6
Waiting · 62

CHAPTER 7
Hiding · 71

CHAPTER 8
Some News! · 86

CHAPTER 9
From the North and to It · 103

CHAPTER 10
An Old Friend and Some New Ones · 122

CHAPTER 11
Elmira · 140

CHAPTER 12
Going Home · 151

CHAPTER 13
A Dreadful Surprise at Bentonville · 159

CHAPTER 14
A Battle—and Peace · 167

Author's Note · 179

CHAPTER 1

Kettle Cousin

K**ETTLE COUSIN, INDEED!** The name stung. Hearing Robert's voice say that stopped Truth Hopkins in her tracks. She stood on the porch behind the partly open door to the kitchen, listening. Cold gusts of the March 1861 wind blew around her. Truth heard her cousin Robert's words clearly, and they were like a stab to the heart. "That's what she is, Ma, a kettle cousin, another mouth to feed. Thee knows what kettle cousins are supposed to do—lick the pot when the rest of us get done with our food. And besides, she can bring us trouble with the law."

"Thy name for thy cousin Truth is cruel, Robert," said Truth's aunt Elizabeth. "It is not her fault or shame she was sent to us with only her carpetbags and what she stood up in.''

Nineteen-year-old Robert was fuming as he went on, ''We didn't get any warning she was on her way from Indiana—only the letter sent along with her by Pa's brother-in-law Hamish saying that he couldn't take her with him to the hospital in California. She's only twelve. He should have left her with some folks back there. And what kind of name is Truth, anyway?''

''It's Tabitha Ruth, as thee very well knows. But we shall call her Truth. As she says, Tabitha Ruth is difficult to say. Remember, she can be a help to me. Thee and Todd will make her welcome and feel a sister to thee. Like thee two, she was reared a Friend. She'll go to the meeting-house with us on meeting day.''

Truth heard Robert's mumbled reply. ''Then make her wear a bonnet. Folks stared at her in Goldsboro when Pa, Todd, and I met her at the train. It's that yellow hair she's got and . . .''

''Yes, I know, Robert. Though she wears our plain dark dress, she stands out. Her hair is butter bright and curly and her cheeks too highly colored. She is a Friend so she will wear a Quaker bonnet. But she is not at fault for the coloring the Lord gave her.''

2

Truth sucked in her breath. Too bright to be a good Friend? What was she to do—get some flour from the bin and dust it on her cheeks to make them pale?

Now, exasperated, Truth set her lips in a firm line. Well, she would show Mister Robert Bardwell she was a faithful Friend and a good, hard worker. She was no stranger to work in houses, gardens, and fields. She could scrub and weed and tend to animals; and she could pick and chop cotton. She was fleet of foot, too. She'd already won two footraces against bigger girls at her new school, and she had attended it only a few days.

Robert spoke again. "I wish she hadn't come. She doesn't know anything about our work."

"Robert, what we do here is done mostly by night. I've taken note that she sleeps heavily. And she sleeps at the front of the house where she can't see what goes on near the barn."

"Ma, do they do the same work in Indiana as we do?"

"Yes, son, but since Indiana is a northern state, perhaps they don't do it as often as we must in the South. I do not think Hamish took part in our work, though. Truth's mother was ill with consumption so much of her life. What we do is done by the strongest of us."

3

"I know that, but our kettle cousin could find out anytime, Ma."

"So she could. If she does, we shall have to put our trust in her. That is all we can do."

Truth heard her aunt sigh. She sounded weary. Aunt Elizabeth's face was long and kindly looking, and her blue eyes were as calm as summer skies. She'd passed on her straight, dark brown hair to her sons, and they resembled her and not her stocky, short, sandy-bearded husband, Matthew, who seldom spoke. Truth liked her. Right now, Aunt Elizabeth was kneading bread dough for the Saturday baking. She was a good farm wife and her husband a good farmer.

Raised on a farm herself, Truth could judge the worth of the Bardwells' North Carolina farm. Their animals were sleek, and their fields of corn and cotton would yield abundantly this summer. Anyhow, she'd show her mother's people how valuable she could be as a farm girl. They'd need no hired girl with her around. She'd do well at school, too, because her aim was to become a nurse someday—but back in Indiana, not in the South. At home, she had heard plenty about the southern states and hadn't liked it a bit, but here she was now. If war

4

came, she would ask to be sent home to some folks who she knew would take her in. That's what Pa had told her to do.

Her forehead creasing in thought, Truth wondered what went on in this peaceful place at night. Would she find out? And why did her being here worry Robert? It must be something dangerous. He had talked about the law.

Truth let out a tiny sigh. Going to a new meetinghouse would be a trial for her. It seemed far easier for old people to behave properly and not fuss and fidget in the silence as they waited for the Inner Light to come to them and inspire them to speak aloud. What courage it would take to dare to speak out, and what confidence in what one had to say. Did the Light have to be grown into, like wisdom? Silly thoughts of running races and climbing apple trees, and sometimes lines of poetry, came flooding into her mind while she sat in the silence. She tried to whisk them away with a mental broom, but they came back to torment her and make her want to smile or laugh and betray by her expression what they were.

From where she stood on the porch, Truth could see her uncle Matthew's broad-brimmed straw hat on its nail by the door. Burning tears sprang to her eyes. It was just like Pa's hat, the one he'd worn in the fields. Pa, Pa! The doctors had told him he needed warmth and dryness for his lungs, so he rented their farm to some neighbors and left for a doctor's sanatorium, a place for sick people, on the edge of the California desert. Truth stifled a sob. No matter how she'd begged Pa, he'd refused to take her with him. No, she hadn't truly been fooled. Pa went out there thinking he would die.

However, he hadn't sent her away penniless, as Robert had claimed. She had twenty dollars in gold knotted in a handkerchief in her bodice. It was her own money. She'd earned it watching children and helping neighbor women in their gardens. This was her secret. If anybody took a stick to her here, that gold would take her away. Pa—how she missed him. He was tall and lanky like Abraham Lincoln, but unlike him Pa was fair-haired and, alas, always coughing, coughing like Mama before she'd died.

"Truth, Truth," came her aunt's soft voice. "Are thee done with getting the eggs from the henhouse? Are thee on the porch now?"

Truth silently stepped some paces backward and then stomped on the boards as if she had just come up the steps, stumbling. Her relations wouldn't like it if they found out she'd been eavesdropping.

"I'm here," she called out. "I got twelve eggs, seven white ones and five brown ones."

Pushing open the back door, she came inside with the basket and laid it on the table beside the empty bread pans. As she came in, she saw Robert go out through the parlor door.

Her aunt said, "The wind in March is cold. Take off thy coat and help me butter the pans. That's a good girl." She smiled. "I hope thee likes it here, child. Thee does not know, but I always hoped to be blessed with a daughter."

"Did thee?" asked Truth, still holding the basket's handle.

"Yes. When I heard of thy birth to my husband's sister, I felt I envied her. My boys were already in school." Finished with her kneading, Aunt Elizabeth turned and asked, "Does thee think thee could become my daughter, Truth?"

Her eyes lowered as she let go of the basket and took off her coat, Truth answered quietly, "I don't know that yet, Aunt Elizabeth."

The older woman laughed. "Thee is rightly named, Truth. Many girls would have said yes to keep the peace. I will be frank, too. We did not anticipate thee coming to us. Thy father did not write. Thy uncle and I are pleased to keep thee. So is thy cousin Todd. However, Robert believes as we do that a war is brewing, and fears thee could be a burden to us when it comes."

Truth said firmly, "I won't be. I can take care of myself."

"I think thee can, and, child, never think thee is a kettle cousin to us."

Truth's head jerked up in surprise, and a flush colored her face. Her aunt knew! "How did thee . . . ?"

"The wind. It blew a wisp of thy hair through the door and then blew it back. Those who eavesdrop will seldom hear good of themselves. Thee is forgiven. There are things thee might have heard Robert say, but put them out of thy head. They do not concern thee."

Truth disagreed, especially if the things had to do with the law. Still, she held her tongue so as not to stir up trouble.

The next day, First Day, or what other people called Sunday, Matthew Bardwell drove his wife, sons, and niece to the meetinghouse. Like her aunt, Truth wore dark clothing and a black, coal-scuttle-shaped Quaker bonnet. In order to see either of their faces, somebody would have had to stoop down and look up inside. Not a single bright strand of Truth's hair showed to shine in the cold March sunshine. The Bardwell men wore their best clothing—white shirts and black suits with black, broad-brimmed hats.

Truth looked about as they took the road leading from the farm. They passed the Bardwells' wide fields on either side. Trees not yet leafed out grew thickly on one side of the road. On the other was the orchard Truth knew consisted of apple and peach trees. She'd been to the root cellar and seen last year's apples still sweet and crisp down there, along with potatoes, pumpkins, and yams. Her home in Indiana had just a loft for storing vegetables.

Sitting behind her in the back of the wagon, Robert and Todd had talked from the moment they had left home. Their voices were soft and not meant to carry over the creak of the wagon and the clopping of the dapple grays' hooves, but Truth's ears were very sharp—too sharp, as Pa had sometimes told her.

Todd, a smaller, thinner copy of his older brother, was saying, "I hear tell that Daniel Fields is coming through Goldsboro pretty soon. He's got himself a coffle almost ready. Wish we could stop him—"

Robert interrupted. "Well, we can't. The law is on his side. I don't plan to see his coffle if I can help it. What road will he take to Virginia? Did thee hear?"

"No. Fields keeps that secret. Just thinking of him gives me a sour stomach, and I don't want it growling at me in meeting."

Robert laughed and began to talk about something else.

Coffle? The word stuck as a question in Truth's mind. She could ask her aunt what a coffle was, but that would surely give away that she'd been eavesdropping again.

Truth sensed things about North Carolina that she didn't understand clearly yet. For one thing, the Bardwell parlor was quite odd. It had the largest fireplace and slab hearthstone she'd ever seen except for one in a tavern in Indiana where a cook's boy turned a spit holding roasting meat. That big fireplace was used for cooking and for heating the room. However, the Bardwells didn't cook in the parlor, and at night the room was heated by a small cast-iron stove. Truth also noticed that there was no watchdog like the dog she'd had at home. How she missed him. It couldn't be that the Bardwells didn't like animals. They had cats. Alice, the calico, even slept on her bed. Yes, there were strange things about North Carolina.

A half hour later, the Bardwell wagon pulled up to the meetinghouse. It was a twin of the one in Indiana—a long, low, unpainted log house, as plain as could be. Truth looked about her carefully. Dark-clad men, women, and children were going into the building. She wondered if anyone here might have known her pa. They'd surely have known her mama, because she'd grown up in this part of the South before she'd met and married Pa. Would there be any girls her own age who were the daughters of her mother's childhood friends? The girls at her new school were Methodists and Baptists. Only two others were Quakers: a plump girl younger than she named Lydia, and a tall, thin girl named Martha, who had given her cross looks when she'd taken off her shoes for the footrace. Back in Indiana, Quaker girls did that sort of thing, but apparently they didn't in North Carolina. Well, she would show them all what kind of Friends were growing up in the West—good ones, strong in their faith and good deeds, and able to do any work they set their hands to.

CHAPTER 2

The Coffle

LIKE ALL THE Quaker meetinghouses Truth had seen, this one, too, was a log cabin chinked with red clay. And like the others, it was divided by a center aisle into a side for men and boys and one for women and girls. The benches were split logs. Set against the front wall under a window was another bench. Three people sat there facing the others, two elderly men in gray at one end and, at the other, an old woman in black with a bonnet bigger than Aunt Elizabeth's. Both old men wore their wide hats, as did the men and boys of the congregation. It was a Quaker mark to keep on the hat. Truth had heard that men of other faiths took off their hats in church while women always wore theirs. She marveled at this.

Truth looked swiftly around. Did she know anybody here? Yes. Two round blue eyes met her dark brown ones from under a bonnet at the end of their bench. It was Lydia, and she was smiling, welcoming her. Truth let out her breath in relief. Lydia was a friend already, it seemed. That was good. She wanted to lean across her aunt and wave, but that would not do at all. She smiled back, and then looked directly ahead and clasped her hands as she should.

The meeting had begun. The meditating had started. Truth bowed her head and tried to clear her mind of her thoughts so she could silently talk with God and hope for his Inner Light. But again, as ever, it was of little use. Images stampeded through her brain—her mama's face, Pa as she'd last seen him, their house, Indiana neighbors, her school, Robert's and her aunt's words about her . . . How she'd like to take up a mop and wipe them away as she would mop a dirty floor. Maybe she never would be able to until she was as old as the woman facing her. In Indiana, only the old people spoke out in a meeting when they had received the Inner Light, never the young ones.

Though it was mostly men who spoke of what they had been gifted to say, sometimes women spoke, too. Truth knew that this made the Society of Friends very unusual, for women had to keep silent in other faiths. Perhaps when she was old, she would speak and be hearkened to.

The meeting went on and on in silence. Truth had no idea how much time had passed. It must have been at least an hour, while the winds blew through the meetinghouse the entire time. The only sounds she heard were a few coughs, one sneeze, and the creaking of the benches as people shifted their weight.

At last, one of the two old men on the front bench rose up and said in a deep voice, "Slavery is a curse on this nation. It must be and shall be stamped out. A war must come and will come. Slavery will be purged by our blood."

The other old man got up next. His voice was a thin wheeze as he said, "Good men have tried to prevent war but have failed. I agree with Friend Moore."

Again there was silence until the second man who had spoken shook hands with the other. After that, everyone got up and shook hands with his or her neighbor. The meeting was at an end.

Leaving with her aunt, Truth was met outside by Lydia Dunn. She came over with two women, who nodded to Truth's aunt. Aunt Elizabeth introduced them as Lydia's mother and grandmother.

Lydia's mother told Truth, "I knew thy mother when she was a girl here, but I never knew thy father. I trust thee and my Lydia will be friends."

"Thank thee. I'd like that," said Truth.

"Come visit us soon, Sister Bardwell, and thee also, Truth."

As Lydia and her family moved away to a waiting wagon, Aunt Elizabeth said, "I see, Truth, thee has made a friend at school."

Truth answered, "Yes, but the other Quaker girl in my class, Martha, doesn't seem to take to me."

"Ah, Martha Buchan? The Buchans do not come to this meetinghouse. They go to another nearer Goldsboro. Their beliefs are somewhat different from ours. All Friends are not exactly alike."

Truth nodded. She had known that. So Martha belonged to a different sect. Some Quakers in Indiana had, too.

"Come, Truth, let's go to the wagon. Thy uncle and Robert are already there. Todd will come soon when he's done with what he has to say to Lucy. Would thee like to sit in the back with the boys?"

Truth looked to her left. Under a tree stood Todd, and close to him was a slender girl in a brown cloak. Truth could tell from the way she tilted her bonnet up to him and he leaned to her that she would be his love. She sighed. Would anybody ever look at her like that?

Though Truth wanted to say to her aunt, "No, I'll sit with thee," she did not. Her aunt wanted her to get to know her cousins better and make friends with them. Her mouth twisted. Robert Bardwell might be a Quaker, but to her he was no friend. His every glance at her told of his resentment. Todd was more easygoing and far more likable. Well, not one word would she pay out to Robert on the way back to the farm.

That night, Truth thought it might snow by morning. In Indiana it would have, but when she looked out her little window at the front of the house in the early light, she saw only a white rime of frost on the road. This was the South. It was cold outside, but the sparkling ice crystals could be gone by midday. There was no wind to bite through her coat and scarves, but all the same she'd best bundle up as if there were.

The three Bardwell men had already breakfasted and gone to the barn to start their chores, so Truth and her aunt ate ham and eggs and biscuits together. The food was very good— better than at home, where she'd done most of the cooking for the past year. Truth had never been able to make biscuits and dumplings properly. Her aunt's were like clouds in the sky. Truth's were like bullets—Pa had even said so.

Bullets! That word made her think of the war that was coming. All Friends were set against wars—they were known for that belief—but they could not stop them. They were peace lovers, not fighters. What would happen if war came? Should she really flee to Indiana? Could she? Would the Bardwells let her? What would happen to Robert and Todd? Quaker men did not go into armies.

Her aunt's words broke into her thoughts. "Do well at school today, child," Aunt Elizabeth said as she walked to the door with Truth.

"Thank thee," Truth answered, and went out with her reader, arithmetic book, and speller, wrapped to the nose in mufflers and a shawl over her coat. No one joined her on the way. Truth followed the road to Goldsboro for a time and then cut across the fields uphill and downhill through several cow pastures.

Her teacher, Michael Hartling, was young, only a few years older than Robert. He was freckled, slender, and had such fine fair hair that he had trouble keeping it out of his eyes. He not only kept the biggest, most troublesome boys busy stoking the black pot-bellied stove, he also ran an orderly school and sure knew his oats when it came to teaching. He never stumbled when he did long division or misspelled hard words. Truth approved of him even if he was not a Quaker.

That day, Lydia came over to her at recess, and they ate their boiled eggs and sandwiches together under a tree. It was still chilly. Truth could see Lydia's breath puff out in the air as she said, "I think Mr. Hartling believes thee to be the best student here. He has said so to my father. He boards with us. He says thee has the makings of a teacher."

Truth mused over this. "I had thought of

being a nurse. There was so much sickness in my house.''

"Thee is homesick for Indiana?"

"Yes." Truth turned her head so the sudden tears that swelled in her eyes didn't show. "My home's there, Lydia."

"Thee cannot go back?"

"No, there is no one there anymore."

"Then stay here with us."

"What else can I do?"

"Thee can visit me someday soon. Our dog has puppies."

Her conversation with Lydia refused to leave Truth's thoughts as she walked back to the Bardwells' house after school. It was still darkening her mind as she came to the road to Goldsboro.

Here her attention was caught by something the likes of which she had never seen before. She heard a strange clinking, jingling noise from around a bend. It was not the familiar sound of a horse's harness. She stood listening at the edge of the road, waiting for whatever it was to come into view.

Her left hand flew up to cover her mouth the instant she saw it—a group of thirteen men, all of them black, chained together four abreast and one alone in front. Few had coats. Some were barefoot. On each side of the column rode white men with pistols in their belts. The man driving the supply wagon carried a whip coiled about his fist. The youngest rider wore a beautiful dark blue coat and a black slouch hat. His mount was a fine bay. He doffed his hat to Truth to show a handsome head of flaxen curls, a ruddy complexion, and fine, even features.

He said, "Stop the coffle, Birnam."

The red-bearded driver shouted, "Halt," and the black men and wagon horses stopped at once.

The young man spoke to Truth. "What do we have here? Ah, a Quaker maid. Why do you stare? Have you never seen a coffle of escaped slaves being taken south where they belong?"

"No, sir," stammered Truth. This was what Tony and Robert had been talking about in the wagon. This was a coffle. It was a dreadful thing.

"I am Mr. Fields from Atlanta. Push back your bonnet so I may see if you have a pretty face."

"No, sir. I don't and I won't. Thee should not ask."

"But I see beneath the bonnet that your hair is like spun gold."

While he laughed at her, Truth fled across the road by the weary group of black men, scooted under a fence, and ran to the shelter of the Bardwell orchards. As she ran, she caught a glimpse of the fugitive slave at the front of the coffle, a tall, thin, light-skinned man who wore the remnants of a good, brown cloth coat and trousers.

Truth ran till her sides ached. Then she collapsed, panting, with her back against an apple tree. Never in her life had she seen anything so horrible. The black men, she knew, had fled to the North to freedom, been tracked down there, and by law were being dragged back into slavery in the South. She'd heard of this in meetings in Indiana when Quakers spoke against it, but never had she seen a coffle until now.

What could she do? She could tell the Bardwells, but they already knew about it, since they had mentioned the name Fields yesterday. She felt sick, so sick she had to hold her stomach to keep down her food. Tears running down her cheeks, Truth bent her head to her knees and waited to feel well enough to go on.

Suddenly, there came a sound, a pounding of feet hitting the cold earth fast. Truth peered around quickly. Could it be her uncle's bull or one of his horses bearing down on her? Could she climb this tree to escape? No, its lowest branches were too high for her to reach. She got to her feet, her schoolbooks spilling from her lap. Now she could see that it was a man coming, his hands balled into fists, his legs pumping. She could hear his labored breathing. It was the slave who had led the coffle. Wrist chains swinging, he ran directly toward her.

Terror overtook Truth. She began to run again. It wasn't far to the house and safety. As fast as her legs could carry her, she made for it through the trees. The slave was following her—chasing her!

Truth reached the front door in a sprint, stumbled up the steps, and yelled, "Aunt Elizabeth! Aunt Elizabeth!" A glance over her shoulder showed her the black man running only twenty feet behind.

Then, thank goodness, her aunt was there at the open door, holding it wide.

"Truth!" she cried as the girl streaked through into the parlor. This was followed by a shout of "Oh, no!" as the fugitive slave darted in on Truth's heels.

CHAPTER 3

Station Six

"TODD, HUSBAND, ROBERT. It's Squire!"

Truth looked on in shock from where she cowered by the hearth while her aunt slammed the front door shut and bolted it.

Then came Matthew Bardwell's voice from the kitchen as he ran into the house. The two boys burst in from the barnyard an instant later. "*Squire!*" cried Uncle Matthew.

As he lay on the floor, the black man gasped out, "They caught me in New York. I busted out of the coffle just down the road from here. Fields will be coming after me with the dogs. Thank goodness he took this road."

"Don't talk, Squire. Save thy wind," ordered Uncle Matthew.

Truth looked on, astounded, as her uncle moved her gently away from the hearth. Then he and her cousins did a very strange thing. They all knelt beside the hearth. Were they praying? No, they were slowly moving the big, flat hearthstone to one side. Beneath it showed a dark pit.

In an instant, Squire had crawled over and squeezed past the stone into the pit. The stone was pushed back into place and the hearthrug placed over it by Aunt Elizabeth.

Still trying to catch her breath, Truth burst out, "He was chasing me!"

"No, he wasn't after thee," said her aunt softly. "He knew where to come because he's been here before. Now he is on his way north to freedom again. There is a tunnel from here to the barn, with air aplenty to breathe. Squire knows what he must do, and so do we."

The truth came to the girl in a flash. She blurted, "Then this is a station on the Underground Railroad?"

"Yes, we hoped thee would never find out," said her aunt. "We were dismayed when someone who did not know about it came here to live."

Truth looked at Robert. "Is that why thee had no liking for me?"

"It is." He gazed levelly at her. "Thee puts a gun to our heads."

Truth protested. "You think I'd tell? I knew a farmer in Indiana who ran a station, too. I was proud to know this. I never said a word to anyone. I am proud of thee. I will not tell."

"See that thee does not."

Now Uncle Matthew spoke up. "The slave catchers will be here very soon. Calm thyselves. Go about thy usual business. Wife, Truth, take up thy mending or knitting. Robert, Todd, go to the barn and stay there. I will meet Mr. Fields when he comes and deal with him. It will be my pleasure." As the boys went out, he sat down in a rocking chair near the hearthstone and put both feet onto the rug.

"We shall knit, thee and I," said Elizabeth Bardwell as she gave Truth the half-knitted scarf she had been working on and took up the four needles and yarn for the stocking she was making. She eyed the girl gravely. "Thee must not tremble and thee must not say a word. Keep thy eyes on thy work. Take off thy bonnet and sit here on the stool at my feet."

As she took off her deep bonnet and heavy outer clothing, Truth asked, "When was the man here before?"

"Ten years ago. He was a house slave in Alabama. He came to us with a young woman, Liley, who was a cook on the same plantation. They planned to marry in the North as free people. Thee knows a slave marriage can be broken and the husband, wife, or children sold at any time."

"How did they catch him?"

"We do not know. We shall ask him when we take him away from here. It would not be easy to capture him. Squire is a clever man. They must have taken him unawares."

"Where will he go if they get hold of him now?" Truth shuddered.

Her uncle answered, "He will either go back to his master or he will be sold. He's strong. They always want strong slaves in the fields. He'd fetch a good sum. A prime hand sells for a great deal of money. It is a foul trade in human souls, and it shall end. It must. It cannot go on longer, though it will surely take a war to stop it."

The three of them grew silent. Truth took

deep breaths to compose herself while she waited. How could her aunt and uncle be so calm? Her heart still raced as she fumbled with her two needles. How could her aunt manage four of them?

The barking of the slave catcher's dogs was their first warning that the men were approaching. Then came a loud knock at the front door and the order, "Open in the name of the United States."

Matthew Bardwell rose slowly, went to the door, and opened it.

On the threshold stood the handsome Mr. Fields, who demanded, "Give up the fugitive slave you've got here. I know you and I've heard about you. You are Quakers. Are you giving shelter to a man who just ran off from me?" His voice was a rasp. "If you are, you are breaking the law of this country, and you will answer for it."

Truth stiffened with fright. She dropped a stitch and fumbled to retrieve it.

Her uncle answered softly, "There is no slave here, sir. Thee may search, but thee will find no one." He went on, "As for thy law, I care nothing for it. We Friends answer to a higher law—

that of God. Come inside if thee chooses and search, but do not disturb my wife and niece with thy vile uproar.''

Truth watched as the man entered. She kept knitting while he walked around, flicking a glance at her as he went by, opening several cupboards and looking inside, and once standing on the very hearth next to Matthew Bard-well's chair. Then he went upstairs, and she heard his footsteps as he went into each of the sleeping rooms. She could hear the barking dogs outside and lifted her head once to see a second man walking about the grounds with them. When he returned to the parlor, Fields gave the Bardwells an angry look. He went through the kitchen to the back door and slammed it shut as he joined his companion.

Aunt Elizabeth smiled at her over her knitting and whispered, ''Squire will be safe. He can hear from down there. Once the barn and other buildings have been searched and the men leave, we shall take care of him.''

''What of the dogs?'' asked Truth.

''They will smell nothing but last autumn's hams hanging in the smokehouse.''

''Where will Squire hide out there in the barn?''

Her uncle interrupted her. "Thee knows enough. Thee need not know everything." He said to his wife, "I will fetch a load of hay to someone we know this evening, and Truth, thee and thy cousins may go with me and ride on the hay. Thee three will make my errand seem innocent. Has thee ever gone on a hayride?"

Truth shook her head. "In Indiana, they say that is for courting."

Uncle Matthew chuckled. "Thee will find this a very interesting ride, too."

Bewildered, Truth bent to the scarf to start a purl row on the patterns. A runaway slave was hiding right beneath them, and her uncle was chuckling and speaking of hayrides before sunset! Besides, a hayride with Robert was not her idea of pleasure. She frowned.

Her aunt's laugh surprised her. "I see that thee does not fancy a hayride to Station Seven on a cold night with Robert. I promise he will treat thee better from now on." Seeing that Truth was still puzzled, the older woman went on, "Thee and our boys and thy uncle will not be the only ones going to Station Seven. They will ride atop the hay. Someone else will ride under it."

Suddenly Truth realized what her aunt

29

meant. Of course! Squire would be under the load, hidden from sight.

Her aunt continued, "I agree with thee, husband. No one would suspect thee if the children went along on this dangerous business." Then to Truth she said, "Niece, the children of Friends here serve the cause, too, and know the risks of the Underground Railroad. Some are even younger than thee. Truth, will thee go willingly? We shall not force thee."

"Yes, Aunt Elizabeth, willingly. I'll go."

"Thee knows if we are caught with Squire, we Bardwells may go to prison and things may fare badly then for thee."

"Yes, I know."

"Good." Her aunt shifted her knitting to one hand and patted Truth's knee with the other. "Thee is a good child, my dear."

Tears welled in Truth's eyes at the loving words. She'd had too few of them recently. Yes, perhaps she could be a daughter to the Bardwells now that she understood Robert's behavior toward her. She'd show her worth not just by sharing hard work but by sharing danger, too.

It took an hour for Daniel Fields, the other

man, and their dogs to satisfy themselves that no runaway slave was hiding on the farm. Standing at the parlor window, Truth saw them leave. Fields's face was dark with anger, and as he passed the window, he shook his fist at her. A sudden flare of rage made her stick out her tongue in return. Slave catchers were brutes.

Another hour passed while the three Bardwell men pitched hay into the back of the big farm wagon and harnessed the team. Then Truth's uncle and cousins came to the house for their warm clothing. Truth was ready, bundled up in her aunt's heavy coat with several shawls over it.

Matthew Bardwell looked at Truth and then at his wife. He said matter-of-factly, "So, she has kept her promise to come with us?"

"Yes, husband."

He nodded and asked, "Is it of thy own free will, Truth?"

"Yes. Is Squire in the hay?"

"Burrowed deep into it," answered Todd solemnly.

Robert added, "He's very weary. He's been on the road in the coffle for weeks. We gave him a warm jacket, a cap, and shoes. We got some of

Ma's hot food into him, too. He'll be all right. At Station Seven, he'll get what he needs to go on to Eight.''

Elizabeth Bardwell said, ''Did Squire tell thee anything of Liley?''

Todd nodded. ''He said they got married by a real preacher up in New York.''

Robert added, ''Squire was a printer's helper in New York City. Slave catchers came inside the print shop and grabbed him. The printer couldn't stop them from hauling him off. Squire says it was good luck Fields took this road south and he'd traveled it before. He'd worked part of his chains free before he got here, and he was ready to run.''

''It wasn't luck,'' avowed Truth's aunt. ''It was God's will working for him.''

''Amen to that,'' agreed her husband.

It was not far from sunset when the Bardwells set out for Station Seven. Perched atop the hay, Truth waved good-bye to her aunt as Uncle Matthew drove the wagon out of the barnyard and onto the road. Beside her sat Todd, and below them was Robert. Because most of the journey would be made by night, two kerosene lanterns occupied part of the driver's seat next to her uncle.

They headed north as Truth had expected—where else would a station be but northward? She asked, "Can Mr. Fields follow us?"

"He could," replied Robert, "but I think he's given up and gone on south of here. We have some neighbors down the road by the name of Gibson who hold with slavery. He'll get a good welcome there, plus whiskey and rest for his horses and coffle. Robert's voice grew bitter now. "The black people are like beef cattle to him and his kind." He spoke down into the hay and asked, "Squire, can thee hear me in there?"

"I heard you," came a deep voice, muffled by the hay. "I heard the girl, too. Tell her I'm sorry I scared her. Can she hear me?"

"I can hear thee," Truth answered. "Thee did frighten me. I didn't understand."

Robert explained, "Truth just came here from Indiana. She didn't know we were conductors on the railroad."

To Truth's surprise, she heard Squire laugh. Then he said, "This is two times you've helped me. I hope I can pay you back, but I don't see how."

Todd asked him, "Up in the North, do they say that war's coming soon, Squire?"

"They truly do—and faster than folks think.

Working with a printer means a person hears a lot of news. The North's shouting for a war now that Mr. Lincoln has been elected."

"And the South's shouting for it, too," Robert replied.

Todd said, "I want to marry Lucy Coxey before it comes. She's willing."

Robert laughed at his brother. "She's been willing since she was eight years old. All thee thinks about these days is love." He said into the hay, "Rest thyself now, Squire. Sleep if thee can. It will be two hours to Station Seven if thee remembers it."

"I recall that."

"Truth, you rest, too," said Todd. He put his arm around her and pulled her closer to him for warmth.

Truth closed her eyes but couldn't truly rest. The cold twilight winds swept over her and right through the coat and shawls. The risks she was taking made her heart beat faster than usual. She opened her eyes as they passed the meeting-house and turned onto another road, still going north. Now they passed carriages and wagons going to and from Goldsboro, and Matthew Bardwell greeted the drivers he knew. No one stopped or spoke long to them. Everyone wanted to get home out of the cold.

At last they came to a farm where a big frame house in a grove of bare-limbed trees stood surrounded by a white picket fence. As they turned into the road leading up to it, a man and woman came out, but no dog rushed to greet them, barking as farm dogs were expected to do. Behind them came a tall girl holding a lighted lantern. With a start, Truth recognized her. Martha Buchan.

William Buchan, thin like his daughter, hailed Truth's uncle. "I see thee has fetched the hay I bought from thee after meeting. Welcome."

Truth thought this had to be a signal. The Buchans had not been at their meetinghouse. In fact, Aunt Elizabeth had said that they went to another. The Buchans knew what a delivery of hay night or day meant, and they were ready. This was Station Seven!

Now she guessed why Martha had treated her so coldly at school. She had acted the same way Robert had, and for a similar reason. From atop the hay, Truth called out to her, "Martha, I

35

came along for the ride. I did not expect to see thee."

Martha lifted the lantern. Her face was pale and strained, but her mouth bent into a grin as she recognized Truth. She called out, "Thee knows?"

"I know, Martha."

Friend Buchan ordered, "Take the hay inside my barn, and we will unload it. Then come to the house for supper. We've had ours, but there's plenty left over in the pot."

"We thank thee, Friend Buchan," said Truth's uncle.

Martha walked along holding the lantern next to the wagon as Matthew Bardwell drove the team to the barn. Truth noticed that Martha's eyes were on Robert, and she knew in an instant that Martha fancied him. Sadly, Robert had given her no more than a brief glance. Probably he figured she was much too young to notice.

Oh, how much she'd learned about her new family in one day! Truth felt truly part of them now. She had let them know where her loyalties lay and had shown her courage. She knew from the quick smile Robert flashed at her in the

Buchan barn that he didn't think of her as a kettle cousin anymore. She smiled at him in return, hoping he could see it from inside the depths of her Quaker bonnet.

CHAPTER 4

Bad Neighbors

AT SCHOOL THE next day, Truth heard news to take home to her aunt and uncle. Towheaded Perry Gibson, who was the same age as she, was the center of attention at recess when he started to tell about the visit Daniel Fields and his slave coffle had made the night before. Perry liked to talk. He even got up on a stump to do it.

As children clustered around him, he said loudly, "I got something to tell you. My pa was sure put out when he heard it. A prime slave got away from Mr. Fields's coffle. That black man they caught up north got loose from his chains and ran like the wind. They went looking for him, but he disappeared, just like that." He snapped his fingers. "That's what Mr. Fields said."

Truth stayed at the back of the little crowd. Lydia came to join her with Martha at her side.

"How could he disappear?" asked a boy.

"Mr. Fields don't know, but he says somebody from around here probably hid him. Why, he even knows who done it. He said that slave was worth four hundred dollars."

"Who did it?" asked a girl Truth had outrun.

Perry looked triumphantly at Truth, Lydia, and Martha. "Them! Them three over there, them Quakers. Mr. Fields says that's what Quakers do. That's what Pa and my big brothers say, too. Quakers hide black slaves we folks own and ship them north. The slaves don't belong to them. Taking them ain't no different from horse or cow stealing. Them Quakers done it!"

"Stand thy ground," whispered Martha to Lydia and Truth. Suddenly she stepped forward and called out, "Slavery's wicked. No man ought to own another man!"

The boy laughed. "Pa says the law says different. So does the Bible. It talks about slavery." He jumped down and walked over to the three girls, followed by a number of boys his age and younger. Standing before the girls, he made a fist and shook it. "If you was boys, I'd fight you good, but you ain't. That don't mean my big brothers can't fight your menfolk."

Her eyes on Perry's fist, Truth said quietly, though her head pounded, "Quaker men don't ever fight, not for any side or any war."

Perry crowed, "If you Quakers won't fight for the South when war comes, your men will get beat up."

"Or burned out!" shouted another boy.

Lydia's frightened cry rose over the cheering that followed. "Mr. Hartling, Mr. Hartling, please come out."

Perry Gibson lowered his fist. Breathing defiance, he whispered, "I wish you three was boys. Just you Quakers wait! Wait till war comes, and you'll get what you been asking for all along. Us good true southerners will come calling on you. Pa vows it."

Martha had the last word before the clot of boys dissolved at Mr. Hartling's appearance in the schoolhouse door. "I bet he vowed it over a barrel of whiskey last night with that slave hunter," she threw at him.

Truth saw how Perry's eyes gleamed like an

angry animal's. They scared her. So did Martha's bravery.

When their tormentors had gone, Truth asked the tall girl in a whisper Lydia wouldn't overhear, "Did Squire get away?"

Martha's nod was grim. "He's at Station Eight by now. Don't ask me where it is. I will not tell thee."

"I would not ask, Martha. Will the Gibsons come to hurt my cousins?"

"Oh, yes, not thy aunt and uncle because they are too old, but Todd and Robert, yes. Some men in Goldsboro once said they'd like to coat them with tar and cover them with feathers. Men die from that."

Truth nodded. She had heard of men who had died in Indiana from that cruelty—good Quakers and abolitionists who weren't Quakers. She asked, "Should I tell my aunt what happened here just now, Martha?"

"Thee need not. Tell her what I told thee of Squire. She knows all she needs to of thy bad neighbors." Martha's eyes were dark and fiery. She asked, "Does thee know the Bible verse, 'Thou shalt not deliver unto his master the servant which is escaped from his master unto thee'?"

"No, I never heard it."

"Thee should know it, Truth. It is in chapter twenty-three of Deuteronomy. If the time comes, say it to slave catchers. We cannot fight with our fists and weapons, but we can with words."

"I'll remember it. Tell it to me again."

That afternoon, Truth kept repeating the verse under her breath, memorizing it, thinking about it. She didn't hear her teacher call on her until he'd called her name twice. He asked, "Woolgathering, Truth?"

"Yes, sir."

"I heard you mumbling. Perhaps you'd like to stand up and tell the rest of us what you find so interesting."

Her face hot with blushes, Truth rose. She said, "It's a Bible verse I just heard. It says . . ."

When she finished, Michael Hartling nodded. "Yes, but keep your mind on decimals. You may sit down."

Truth was aware of her teacher's level look at her as she was speaking. It made her feel he approved of her words. Yet she was also aware of Perry Gibson's snickering.

42

* * *

March passed with more and more talk of a war brewing. The Bardwell men returned long-faced from their trips to Goldsboro. Truth noticed how her aunt watched for them to come back each time from the front porch. Once Todd came home with a black eye and bruised face and would say only that he had met a Gibson in town. Twice on rainy meeting days, clods of wet earth were hurled at the meetinghouse, thudding against the walls. No Quaker went out to see who threw them.

Truth loved springtime. Though the Bardwells kept just a few cows and no sheep, catching sight of the baby calves delighted her. One morning in mid-April, she stopped on her way to school to watch them in the field they shared with their mothers. The babies' clumsiness enchanted her. One little black-and-white bull calf was getting to know her and would come to the fence to have his muzzle scratched when he was not suckling. She had named him Blackberry after a calf she and her father had had back home. Each time she saw him, she thought of Indiana.

Why hadn't Pa written? Was he too sick? She'd written him twice. Letters took so very long to get from North Carolina to California, weeks and weeks. Perhaps one was on its way?

While she stood outside the rail fence near the great pile of gray boulders that marked the northern edge of the pasture, she heard the quick thud of hooves. Truth looked up. The rider galloping toward her on a bay horse was her enemy, Perry Gibson, who rushed past, almost knocking her down.

He reined in, shouting, "The South fired on Fort Sumter in South Carolina with the Yankees inside it. Pa just found out. That ain't so far from here. The war's starting. Tell old man Hartling I won't be at school today. I'm on my way to Goldsboro."

Perry threw back his head and cheered, and then set his heels to the bay and shot past her.

Once he was out of sight, Truth squared her shoulders and headed for the house. Yes, she'd have to pass on the news about Fort Sumter. The Bardwells had expected something like this to happen. Uncle Matthew had said it would be the first step toward war.

"Why has thee come back, Truth?" her aunt asked her when she came into the kitchen.

"There's news."

After Truth told what she had heard, the

woman sighed, wiped soapy water off her hands, and said, "I will tell the men. Get thee to school. This is not a holiday."

"There'll be a war now, won't there?"

"Oh, yes, child." Aunt Elizabeth gave her a little smile. "Do not expect to hear the war much spoken of in this house. We shall try to take no part in it. Go tell the teacher and the Friends thee knows at school what that boy told thee. Do not be angry at him."

Truth cried, "He's hateful. That's so hard, Aunt Elizabeth."

As the woman took her shawl from a nail and flung it over her head, she said, "The way of a Friend can be hard. Not all who call themselves Friends will remain strong in this war."

"But we will, won't we?"

"Yes, we shall, dear."

Little was said about the news at supper that April night, except at the end of the blessing before they started to eat. Then Matthew Bardwell added, "Thou shalt not kill! That is what we live by."

While she ate, Truth thought of what had happened at school that day. She had not been the first with Perry's news. Someone had brought it earlier. Most of the children whose parents wanted a war ran about happily, shouting, wrestling, and leaping on one another. Finally Mr. Hartling dismissed the school and sent the children home. Truth and the other Friends stayed behind somberly at their desks.

Martha Buchan asked boldly, "What will thee do, Mr. Hartling? Will thee go to be a soldier for the South?"

His face was troubled as he replied, "I don't know yet, Martha."

Lydia said, "Thee is a Methodist. My mother says Methodists go to war."

Michael Hartling frowned. "We may dance and have parties, but not all Methodists go to war."

Lydia spoke again. "Papa says soldiers from this state can come take thee to be a soldier, too. South Carolina left the Union just before Christmas. Papa says this state will secede shortly."

"That's true." He smiled a little. "But it will take time to do that. War has not even been declared yet."

"Will thee stay here till then?" asked Truth, who to her surprise found that the thought of his going to war was as dreadful as if he'd been a Friend.

"Yes, Truth, as long as I can. I do not want to leave here." He gave her a wide smile.

Truth grinned back, warmed by his reply.

Martha said, "We hope all will go well with thee."

"Thank you. Well, you'd best go home, too. Be careful. You Quakers won't be well-liked in the South right now."

"We know that," agreed Lydia.

That night, the Bardwells experienced their first taste of trouble. A whooping band of horsemen came galloping down their road from their evening of celebrating in Goldsboro. As they went by, a shower of rocks clattered against the front of the house.

The noise awakened Truth. She went out onto the landing and saw her cousin Robert in his long nightshirt. He was leaning out the hall window where the glass had shattered. She heard him tell his brother, who had joined him, "It's the Gibsons going home. They've been drinking in some Goldsboro tavern. We'll either have to get the glazier to repair the glass in the window or board it over."

"Board it over is best," said Todd. "They'll be back."

CHAPTER 5

War Comes

TWO DAYS LATER, Truth was awakened in the middle of the night by the scraping, grating noise of the big hearthstone being moved and pushed back into place. She smiled into the dark. Another escaped slave had reached Station Six.

The next morning at breakfast, she asked her aunt and uncle, "I heard the hearth last night. Who came to us?"

Her uncle answered, "A woman the Gibsons held as a slave. She'd been whipped badly. She left here before dawn with Robert. He is upstairs sleeping. I guess thee did not hear him come in. The woman was a house slave, not a field hand, so her absence will be noticed quickly. But she is far away by now. Eat and get thee to school. If the Gibsons come here, we shall deal with them. Thee need not be here."

"I will stay if thee wants me to."

Her aunt smiled. "We know that, but we have no need of thee."

On her way to the path to her school, Truth was met by four Gibsons on horseback, the heavy-bodied, gray-bearded father and three of his four big, towheaded, pale-eyed sons. Perry was not with them. She reckoned he'd gone to school.

They reined in just ahead of the great boulder pile in the pasture. Sam Gibson, a red-faced man in a long black coat, asked her harshly, "Quaker gal, have you seen a black female of thirty or so anywhere around here?"

"No, sir, I have not." That was no lie. Truth had not seen her.

He scowled. "I can't see your face in that bonnet, so I can't tell if you're lying. That slave's called Abigail, and she has run away from me. She needs another whipping, one she'll never forget. We think she came here to the Bardwells. A man we know named Fields says you all run a station on that Underground Railroad."

Truth hesitated, then said, "Mr. Fields came to my uncle's place hunting a poor black man who got away from him. I was there when he came. He had dogs with him. They searched all over but didn't find anyone." Again, this was no lie.

One of the Gibson boys, who had a pug nose and checked coat, snorted. "That's because he was hidden away real good. Pa, there ain't no use talking to this gal. I bet she don't know much, anyhow, because she's so new here. She even talks Yankee-like. Folks running that railroad probably wouldn't let her in on it."

Sam Gibson grunted. "We can't beat it out of her even if she does know. She's a gal. Maybe you got it right, Hank. We'll look around some on the roads. Then we can double back and have a talk with these here Bardwells. 'Friends,' they call themselves." He laughed. "Fine friends they are to the South—slave stealers."

It was on the tip of Truth's tongue to say, "That's better than being slave catchers," but she held in the words.

Another of the Gibson boys pointed to the boulder heap on the Bardwell property. "Your uncle ain't much of a farmer to keep that pile of rocks around. He could be farming the land under it. It ain't doing him no good there. Ain't that right, Lockwood?"

"We're wasting time, boys," said the elder Gibson. "The longer we sit here and talk, the farther away Abigail gets. She's fleet of foot. She cost me a pretty penny when I bought her. Let's get going."

Without another word, he set spurs to his large sorrel horse and started off, followed by his sons.

Biting her lip, Truth continued on her way to school. So they thought she was of too little consequence to know what went on. Well, let them think that. It was safer that way, wasn't it? Besides, pretty soon it would be just old Mr. Gibson, Perry, and their slaves at the Gibson place. The three big sons would go into the Confederate army. Aunt Elizabeth had said that Mrs. Gibson had died last year, probably worn out from serving the Gibson men. It was hard to feel sorry for Perry and his pa, they were so spiteful. Abigail had probably been the one to keep house for them all. She had most likely been overworked and whipped plenty at their place.

Truth smiled in the depths of her bonnet as she went onto the path to school. Wouldn't it be fine if all their slaves ran away?

With April came the spring plowing. Truth went into the fields to watch the plowshare drawn by the horses turn the dark earth. She'd always enjoyed watching this in Indiana, but seeing it now made her think of her father. Why hadn't Pa written? She'd written to him every week without fail.

While the Bardwell men planted twenty acres of corn and fifteen of oats, Truth and her aunt planted a vegetable garden behind the house in a fenced-off area safe from the chickens. This was work Truth enjoyed. She loved to see the tiny green seedlings rise up out of the ground.

She took over the chore of mixing the swill for the hogs and putting it into their troughs. She knew to keep well away from the three sows with their spring litters of wriggling little piglets. Sows had uncertain tempers as well as sharp teeth.

*　*　*

The letter Truth had been waiting for came in mid-May. Todd brought it from Goldsboro. To her surprise, the address was not in her father's handwriting, though the letter had come from California. Opening the envelope, she saw that the letter was from one of the doctors at the sanatorium. It said:

My dear Miss Hopkins,

I regret to inform you that your father has passed away. It was a peaceful passing. He had given us your address and asked that I write to you when I must. He knew it was to happen. I am most sorry to tell you this. If it comforts you, he did not complain of any pain, and he seemed to feel that you were in safe hands with your mother's people in North Carolina. The prospect of a civil war alarmed him, as it does all of us. However, he knew he had no other place to send you.

He is buried here in our cemetery. His grave will be well tended, I assure you. I enclose a lock of his hair for you. He said you might want it. Your father spoke often of you and called you a brave girl. He thought very highly of you.

Sincerely,
Amos Harrah, M.D.

Truth let the letter fall and sat down on the top step of the front porch. She stared at the lock of light brown hair until her aunt came out of the front door. Silent tears flowed down Truth's cheeks.

"Todd tells me he brought thee a letter from California. I see from thy face it is bad news. Come here now, my dear child." The woman sat down beside her and drew her into her arms. While Truth sobbed, Aunt Elizabeth said, "Cry, cry, little one. Let it out. It must be that thy father died."

Truth gasped out, "Yes. He is dead. His doctor sent me a lock of his hair."

"That was kind of him. I have a silver locket thee can put it in. A friend who is not a Quaker once gave it to me. I kept it even though we wear no jewelry. It will not show under thy dress, Truth. Thee knows now about thy father."

Truth buried her head in her aunt's shoulder. She cried out, "How can the sun shine when Pa's dead and there's a war coming?"

Elizabeth Bardwell did not answer. Instead, she started to rock back and forth, holding Truth, patting her shoulder while they wept together. "I will need thee now, Truth. I will need

54

thee because I must soon lose Robert and Todd. Thee shall be all I have—and doubly precious to me."

A few days later, North Carolina seceded, joining the Confederacy on May twentieth. Truth heard the news at school when a rider pelted past the schoolhouse shouting, "The state's seceded. North Carolina left the confounded Union!"

Mr. Hartling's classroom erupted with noise. Perry Gibson jumped atop his desk and jigged. Other boys copied him until the teacher shouted at them to sit down. Then, knowing that nothing would be learned that day, he dismissed school.

Although the other students were only too happy to leave, Truth, Lydia, and Martha stayed behind to talk with Mr. Hartling. Lydia asked, "What will happen next?"

He told her somberly, "The state militia will become soldiers for the Confederacy. At first, the army will be all volunteers. Then if the war lasts, there will probably be conscription."

"What's that?" asked Martha sharply.

"Able-bodied men will be forced into the

army. That may take a while to happen, though." Mr. Hartling looked out the window. "I'll stay here until then."

Truth asked, "Will they try to take Friends, too?"

"Oh, yes. I'm sure they'll want all young and strong men. The Bardwells know that very well." He glanced at the black band on her right sleeve and added, "You've had a lot to bear lately, Truth, with the death of your father. Maybe you should have stayed in Indiana. That state will stay in the Union."

Lydia told him, "My pa says the Union will probably want Quaker men, too."

"I'm afraid that's a fact."

Martha's face was drawn tense as she turned to Truth and asked, "What will your cousins do? What will happen to Todd and Robert?" Her voice lowered as she spoke Robert's name.

Truth told her softly, "I think they decided that some time ago. First of all, I think Todd will marry Lucy Coxey. Robert has no true love that I know of." She managed a smile for Martha.

The First Day meeting the following week was the most thrilling one Truth had ever attended. Many Friends stood up and spoke, and afterward Todd and Lucy were wed. Truth watched Todd in his dark suit and broad-brimmed hat come to sit with the Bardwells. Then he and Lucy in her gray-green dress and black silk bonnet stood up before all. Todd put a plain gold ring on Lucy's finger, and after that, the couple remained standing while all the people in the meetinghouse signed their wedding document one by one. Todd's face shone with happiness, and Truth was sure that in the depths of her bonnet, so did Lucy's.

Truth sighed as she added her name. She knew that Todd and Lucy would have almost no time together. Todd would have to flee and so would Robert—and very soon. The summer reaping of the oats would have to be done by their father alone or with the aid of the other Quakers. No Confederate farmer would help him.

Truth awoke to wild shouting Monday night and sat up in bed in terror. A glance through her window showed her the road filled with horse-men carrying lighted torches. This time it wasn't just the Gibson men. A dozen or so others, strangers to her, were with them.

She caught the shout of one loud-voiced rider. "We come for you quaking Quaker cowards. We're militia. Tomorrow we're all joining the Confederate army. Come on out and join us."

She heard her uncle's reply, "We'll do no such thing."

"You want us to burn you out here and now?" bellowed Hank Gibson.

Truth watched in horror as he raised his torch high and shook it to make sparks fall.

"We could set fire to your barn. We hear Todd just got married. Tell him to fetch out the bride so we can give her a hug and a kiss."

Matthew Bardwell's voice rose over the clamor. "My son and his wife are not here in this house, I'm happy to say."

"Then fetch out your old woman and the young gal you got, the pretty one with the yellow hair. We'll kiss them instead. We don't care if they come out in their nightgowns, just so long as they don't wear them big black bonnets of theirs."

Anger flooded Truth. She flung open the window, leaned out, and shrieked, "Here I am! Thee can have a look at me. Does it please thee to wake us up at midnight? Is this how southern

58

men treat women? I am not wearing a bonnet. Now go away. I am ashamed of thee!"

Another Gibson boy, Lockwood, yelled, "We could come up, missy, and haul you down and spank you."

Sam Gibson's voice thundered out, "That ain't the way southern men treat women, and you know it, son. You got a look at her. If Bardwell says Todd and the Coxey gal ain't here, we'll never find them. It'll be like looking for slaves like Fields done—wasting our time. We got other places to go tonight. I warn you though, Quaker, next time we come, we might come with a pot of hot tar and some feathers. Let's go, men."

Truth drew back and peeped from behind the curtain. She saw him rein his bay about and start north along the road. The others followed. A moment later, her aunt was there to hold her. "That was very bold of thee—but foolish, girl. They could have come inside."

Robert entered her room, too, carrying a candle. He said, "I do not know how thee knew what to say, but thee said just the right thing to make them go away. How did thee know?"

His mother answered, "The Lord must have prompted her. Did thee feel the Light? Southern men are proud of their respect for women, but how would thee know that, Truth?"

"I didn't know. The words just came to me," said Truth, shivering. Yes, she'd been bold. "Will they come back tonight?"

Her aunt replied, "No, they'll probably go to other Quaker farms, perhaps to the Dunns'. Robert, get dressed and saddle thy horse. Fetch Todd back here. He and Lucy are staying in the cabin behind the Coxey house at their farm near Bentonville. Have him ride back with thee. The two of thee must leave here before daybreak."

"Yes to that," added Matthew Bardwell as he came stamping up the stairs in his long white nightshirt. "While thee rides to bring Todd home, we'll get everything ready for thee to take to Canada."

"Canada?" cried Truth.

Robert answered, "Canada probably won't come into the war. We'll be safe there. That's where runaway slaves are safest, too, from the slave catchers, though some of them stay in the northern states." In the candlelight, Truth saw his face was grim. "The North would take us as soldiers as fast as the South, once conscription begins. We don't know when that time will come."

Saying this, Robert turned swiftly and left the room.

Elizabeth Bardwell told Truth, "We'll get food and extra clothing ready for the boys to put in their saddlebags. Come down with me now."

"I'll get dressed and get money for them from the secret place," said Matthew Bardwell. "A hundred dollars in gold and silver should take them there. They can sell the horses in the North and take the railroad to Canada."

CHAPTER 6

Waiting

Todd and Robert came riding home an hour before daylight. While their horses were carefully readied for a long and fast journey by their stern-faced father, the young men swiftly ate a huge breakfast of ham, eggs, and hominy grits. Meanwhile, Truth and her aunt packed their saddlebags with sandwiches, jackets, trousers, rainproof coats, and changes of underclothing.

Little time was wasted on farewells. Robert had told his brother of the night's threatening visit by the Gibsons and their friends. They both knew the men would be back if he and Todd stayed.

Todd said very little, and spoke only once of

his wife. "Lucy says I have to go. She'll come here to live with thee, Ma and Pa, anytime thee need her."

"Her own mother needs her right now," said Elizabeth Bardwell firmly. "We shall see her as often as we can."

Robert put in, "We can't write, but we will send messages. Thee knows how."

Truth's uncle nodded. "Through our special railroad, the Buchans. Now, here is fifty dollars for each of thee." Truth saw the bright coins shake into his palm from a leather sack. He divided them between his two sons. "Take our blessings and go. May God keep thee safe. Remember thy faith."

The older Bardwells embraced their sons, and then Truth was swung off her feet and caught up in a strong embrace, first by Todd, then Robert.

Robert whispered in her ear, "I was proud of thee last night. Keep up thy courage. I am glad thee has come. Thee will be a comfort here."

"And I am proud of both of thee," she told him.

Robert and Todd now mounted their horses, lifted their hats and left at a fast trot.

A moment later, Truth heard the thud of

hooves on the road that led north. She looked at her aunt and uncle. Their faces were gray and tense in the pale dawning.

Her uncle Matthew said, "I must ride out and tell members of our faith what has gone on here. There are other young men who should leave us now." He went toward the barn.

Elizabeth Bardwell turned away from watching the empty road and told Truth, "Thee need not go to school today. Thee and I will take up the rag carpets and beat them. Then we shall make whitewash for the walls and ceilings. It is best to be busy. Work takes the thoughts from trouble. Has thee ever made whitewash?"

"No."

"It is made with lime, flour, laundry bleach, and boiling water. Go upstairs and put on thy oldest clothing."

Truth, her aunt, and her uncle went to the First Day meeting as usual the next week. There, Truth Hopkins had another shock.

Everything went as always until a tall, young Quaker suddenly stood up, cleared his throat, and said, "I find it in my heart to speak to thee."

Truth gasped and stared at him along with everyone else but his parents, who sat slumped forward. He could not have been any older than Todd. He was by far the youngest person she had ever heard speak out at a meeting.

He was silent for a long moment, and then he said in a harsh, husky voice, "I cannot find it in my soul to fight for the South and slavery. Nor can I find it there to go to Canada. Yes, I will go north, but I'll go to offer myself to the army of the Union in Maryland or Pennsylvania. I will serve the North as a soldier."

He didn't wait to hear what might be said. He walked stiffly, awkwardly, out of the meeting-house, with his parents following him. Truth's eyes watched them through the window until she felt her aunt's arm on her sleeve. It was then she remembered having heard that not all Quakers refuse to fight.

Now the waiting began—waiting to hear from Todd or Robert. No news came either by way of other Quakers who traveled about more or by the Underground Railroad that could send letters as well as human beings.

June came, bringing warm days and no school. Matthew Bardwell cultivated his corn, weeding the fields with the help of his farm machinery. After he finished with that, he went on to cut logs for a new corncrib and to arrange with other Quakers to help him harvest the oat crop in late summer.

Truth and her aunt began to can pickles from garden cucumbers, and pick wild berries to make jams and jellies. With her cousins gone, Truth did their chores as well as her own.

"Thee is a great help and comfort to us, Truth," her aunt told her often. Then she would sigh and look out the nearest window, letting Truth know she longed to see her sons come riding home. But Elizabeth Bardwell knew as everyone else did that they would not. The war was not going away as everyone had hoped. More and more of the Bardwells' non-Quaker neighbors left home to join the Confederate forces.

The Bardwells' acquaintances were now aware that their two sons had left, and they guessed at their destination. Sometimes riders passing in the night would shout "Cowards!" and "Canada!" and throw stones to rattle on the roof, but in general they kept their distance. Truth and her aunt stayed away from Goldsboro, where Quakers were spat at on the street and were shoved by passersby. Some merchants refused to sell Matthew Bardwell any goods.

* * *

On the second day of July, news came to the Bardwells that left them white-faced with horror. An old Quaker traveling from Virginia arrived at the farm with Martha Buchan's tall, gaunt father. The two men spoke first in the road with Matthew Bardwell and then came into the house.

From the grim expression on her uncle's face, Truth could tell the stranger brought evil news. Matthew Bardwell said, "Robert and Todd were caught in northern Virginia."

Truth ran to her aunt's embrace, crying, "Oh, no!"

"Friend Buchan, tell us," asked Elizabeth Bardwell softly.

The Quaker motioned to the old man next to him. "Friend Hall will tell thee. He saw it happen."

The man's round pink face was sympathetic, but his words were dreadful. "I live near Winchester on a highroad. A few weeks ago, I was repairing my fence when two young men, thy sons, stopped to ask me the way. While we were talking, Virginia cavalrymen in gray uniforms came out of the woods on the other side of the road. There were at least twenty of them." He

67

spread his hands in a gesture of helplessness. "Thy sons were taken. I heard the captain say they would be forced into the Confederate army no matter what state they came from. He said, 'Quakers can make good cannon fodder. That's about all they're good for.' Then he laughed. They took thy lads away. Before they left, one of them told me his name and where thee lived, and asked me to let thee know. My wife was ill, but she's better now. I came as soon as I could."

"We thank thee, Friend Hall," said Truth's aunt sadly. "Would thee and Friend Buchan take supper with us?"

"Thank thee, yes. But that is not all, Sister Bardwell," added William Buchan. "Unfortunately, thee must know the rest. I have heard that there's to be a battle soon. It is said it will be in northern Virginia."

Aunt Elizabeth put her hands to her mouth to stifle a moan as Truth cried, "Will Todd and Robert be in it?"

The old man nodded. "It could be that they will take part. Only God knows that."

On the twenty-first of July, the Union and Confederate armies met near Manassas Junction in Virginia, not far from Washington, D.C.

What the North had expected to be an easy victory turned into a shameful rout. Foolish, overconfident picnickers from Washington had come out to watch what they considered to be a show, but they hastily turned their buggies and wagons around and sped to safety.

News of the battle reached the Bardwells in North Carolina two weeks later. Men and women spoke of it with horror at the First Day meeting, and Truth knew by the look on her aunt's and uncle's faces what they were thinking, fearing.

Truth went to bed early with her muscles aching from a long day spent stirring laundry boiling in a great pot on a hot, mid-August day. Smoke from shifting winds had made her eyes burn and she wanted to rub them, even though her aunt warned her not to. She was still awake, trying not to put her fists to her eyes, when she heard the rumble of wagon wheels outside and a muffled "Whoa." Another slave for the Underground Railroad? she wondered. None had come for a while.

This time was different, though. Truth heard her aunt's quick footsteps on the stairs, and a minute later she was in her little room.

Aunt Elizabeth's words came out in a furious rush. "Truth, Truth, it's Todd. He's come home. Come downstairs quickly. We need thy help. He has escaped from the Confederates, but he's hurt. He has a bullet in his leg. He was in that battle. We must hide him."

As Truth scrambled out of bed and put on her brown calico wrapper, she asked, "How did he get here?"

"From Station Seven with Friend Buchan. He was sent along south from Station Eight in Virginia."

CHAPTER 7

Hiding

Truth would not have known her cousin Todd if she had passed him on the street in Goldsboro. He was bearded now and very thin, and his sunken eyes were bleary and reddened. He didn't wear a gray uniform or Quaker clothing but a dirty, poor-fitting black-checked coat and trousers. Todd sat in one of the kitchen chairs with his leg propped up on the seat of another. His father knelt beside him and slit the seam of the trousers with a knife. A tattered rust-colored bandage circled his left calf just below the knee.

Todd gasped out, "The bullet chipped the leg bone and stayed inside the flesh. A Friend took me to a doctor in Virginia who got it out. Did the best he could, he said, but it still hurts. I feel hot."

"Rest easy, son. We'll get you well," said Matthew Bardwell comfortingly. "Elizabeth, feed Todd and Friend Buchan while I fetch a lantern and get a place ready for Todd. It would be best for him to stay at the Rocks, not in the barn."

At the Rocks? Truth shook her head. What could that be?

"Yes, the Rocks," agreed her aunt. "Husband, take the bedding from his and Robert's beds and set it out. And leave a lantern with him tonight. I'll get the stove stirred up and make coffee and sandwiches. Truth, get a cloth and soap and a clean towel for Todd's wound."

"I'll clean the leg," volunteered William Buchan. "I worked for a doctor once. I brought him here the minute he came to us."

"We thank thee," said the elder Bardwell as he went out to the rear of the house.

Truth hurried ahead of her aunt to the kitchen, found a towel and the yellow soap her aunt had made, and got some water from the kitchen pump. By the time she returned, William Buchan had the bandage off. Truth saw the red wound that was festering yellow, and no-

ticed how her cousin flinched when Friend
Buchan dabbed at it with soap and water.

To take his mind off the pain, she asked
Todd, "Did thee have to be a soldier?"

"No. No, I never was. We never got uniforms. They dressed Robert and me in clothes
like this and pushed us ahead to the front of the
battle. We both lay down in the grass, but no
matter. It was a Yankee who shot me. I'll never
forget . . ." His voice trailed off.

"Thee did not have a rifle, did thee?" asked
Truth.

Todd laughed without humor. "No, nothing
but our bare hands."

"They *wanted* thee killed?" cried Truth.

"Looks that way, doesn't it. They said that
was all we Quakers were good for."

Wincing as the bandage was wound around
his calf, Todd went on, "After the Confederate
cavalry caught us, they tried to get us to learn to
be soldiers, but we wouldn't. To make us
change our minds, they didn't feed us enough.
They made us stand on a barrel tap for a long
time, and trussed us up with ropes like turkeys
and left us out in the hot sun all day without
water. They made us carry logs on our shoulders for hours and hours till we ached all over,

but we wouldn't ever say yes to soldiering. That's when they gave up on us. And when they found out there was going to be a battle, they shoved us out in front dressed like this.''

"Where's Robert?" Truth asked tearfully.

"I don't know. Martha Buchan asked, too, but I couldn't tell her, either. There was gunpowder smoke all over the battlefield. It sure stank. It was thick, and it was always moving. Sometimes thee could see the men around thee, and sometimes thee couldn't. When I got shot, I saw Robert on the grass. Then a soldier lifted me up and pulled me away and piled me against a fence, and I lost sight of him. Maybe the Confederates still have him. Maybe he got away by himself. Lots of men were running in all directions. The South won. Did thee hear that, Truth?''

"Yes, we heard. How did thee get off the battlefield?"

"I crawled under that fence and got into a pasture that had a little ditch at one end. It was full of weeds and water. I rolled down into it and stayed there till the battle was all over. Nobody came hunting for me. Guess they didn't care, or they got too busy and forgot. The farmer found me that night. He could have turned me in to the army, but he didn't. He said a Quaker had done him a favor once. His wife used to be a nurse, and she fixed me up some. When I told them who and what I was, they took me to some Quakers they knew. They got a doctor to take out the bullet. I just wanted to come home, so as soon as I was feeling a little better, the Friends started me back here on the Underground Railroad from a station they knew about."

Todd flexed his leg, moaned, and said, "Truth, will thee ride to the Coxeys in the morning and let Lucy know I'm back and where I am?"

"Yes, yes, I will, Todd. But will she know where to come? What's the Rocks?"

"It's a cave in the rocks in the cow pasture. It's pretty big. That's where a few slaves are hid when they come to us. We don't do that often, though. We keep the rocks even more secret than the hearthstone."

By now, Truth's aunt had returned with cold water for her feverish son and a plate of roast beef sandwiches. She said, "The coffee will be ready soon. Eat and rest, Todd. Thee, too, Friend Buchan. We owe thee Buchans much."

"I asked Truth to ride over to tell Lucy to-morrow," Todd said.

"Yes, that will be done. Rest till thy father and Friend Buchan take thee to the Rocks. Tell me about thy brother. Did he get away, too? Where is he?"

Todd drank and then said, "Like I told Truth and Friend Buchan, he was in the battle, too, but after I was wounded, I lost sight of him. I don't know what happened to him. I told the farmer who found me how he was dressed, and he went out looking for Robert. But he never found him."

William Buchan said softly, "That means he could have run off to the North"—his voice faltered—"or the Confederate army's still got him."

Elizabeth Bardwell's face twisted in grief. "Or he's dead?"

"No, Ma, he isn't dead. That farmer looked at the dead men. There wasn't anybody dressed the way he was, just like me. Twins must have worn these outfits."

"Thank God for how thee was dressed. Thank God for that good Virginian. Bless him."

"Amen to that," came from Friend Buchan.

An hour later, Truth and her aunt followed her uncle and Friend Buchan as the men helped the limping Todd through the cow pasture. They headed for a pile of great boulders, skirted them, and stopped at a place where a lighted lantern had been set on the ground. Trailing vines covered the face of one jagged rock. As Matthew Bardwell pushed the vines aside, Truth saw a cleft in the rock just wide enough for a person to pass through. One by one, they entered and stood in the good-sized cavern. Another lantern stood on a table in the center, and a crude bed was set in a corner. It was piled high with old quilts. There were some stools scattered about and two wooden benches. Todd was led to the bed, eased down on it, and covered with quilts by his worried-looking mother.

"I'll stay with my boy tonight," said Elizabeth Bardwell, going over to sit down on the stool beside the bed. It was a signal for the rest of them to leave.

As Truth turned away, Todd called out to her, "Be sure to tell Lucy as soon as thee can. Ask her to come as soon as she is able."

"Oh, yes, Todd. I will." She looked into her uncle's solemn face and softly asked, "Will soldiers come here looking for Todd?"

"Most likely they would have looked for their dead on that battlefield. They'll hunt down deserters the way the slave catchers do. That's what they'll call Todd even though he never joined up. But they won't find him.''

Matthew Bardwell's expression grew more grim. "It would be wisest for Todd to go away again for as long as the war goes on, and that could be years. But he can't travel the way he is now.''

"When he gets well, can he help us with the harvest?''

"No, child. He can come out only at night. He's a Confederate deserter. He can't be seen outside in the daylight unless the Union army takes over this state. But who knows about them? They might try to make him a soldier for their side.''

"That's terrible . . .'' Truth began to cry, but her uncle took her by the elbow and led her and William Buchan outside.

"Todd does not need thy pity. He must keep up his courage—and regain his strength. Thy wailing will do him no good. Seem brave for his sake!'' He spoke next to his neighbor. "I need not tell thee to keep this place secret. Do not tell thy wife or daughter.''

"No, they will not hear of it.''

Truth left her uncle's side to tug at the other

man's sleeve. When he turned to her, she whispered, "Friend Buchan, please tell Martha that Todd thinks Robert is alive."

"I shall tell her."

"Come, Truth," ordered her uncle. "You need to sleep if you can. I'll saddle a horse for thee in the morning to ride to Bentonville and the Coxeys. Does thee ride well?"

"They told me so in Indiana. Papa kept a saddle horse, a mare." Truth hesitated before she added, "Uncle, I rode astride in Indiana, as a boy does. Sometimes I didn't even have a saddle."

"No saddle?" Uncle Matthew stopped in his tracks. "That was Indiana, child. Here thee will ride on thy aunt's sidesaddle. Can thee manage that? Thee will be seen on the road. Thy aunt would not approve of all thy father let thee do in Indiana."

Truth sighed. No, she would not. But it had been very pleasant to ride with her hair unbound, flying behind her in the wind. Oh, how hard it was to be a Friend!

A little after sunrise, Truth's uncle hoisted her into her aunt's sidesaddle. Her mount was a lively little bay gelding called Hosea. He was gentle and surefooted, and a joy to ride in the cool early morning. She met few people. They were all strangers to her, but pleasant enough in their nodded greetings. She knew the way to Bentonville from a wagon journey she'd taken to visit the Coxeys soon after Todd's marriage. Bentonville was only a cluster of small houses a morning's swift ride from the Bardwell farm. The Coxey house was more imposing than any other in the hamlet—larger than the Bardwells' and finer than anything Truth had yet seen in North Carolina. Friend Coxey was a prosperous man who owned broad fields. The sturdy-looking house had two stories and was sided with clapboards. There was a shady veranda at the front for hot-weather sitting. Behind the house were sheds and a barn, corncrib, and smokehouse, but these were larger than the Bardwells'. Handsome horses came running from their rich pasture to greet Truth's horse.

Their nickering brought Sister Coxey and Lucy out onto the veranda to see who had come. When the two women recognized who it was, they ran down the steps. Truth saw how drawn their faces had suddenly become, as if they feared her news.

She reined Hosea in, leaned over from the

saddle she'd found a very slippery, awkward perch, and told them, "It's Todd. He's come back. He was in that battle at Manassas and got hurt, but he'll be all right. We're hiding him. My uncle says he's safe. Todd sent me. He wants thee to come back with me, Lucy."

"Yes, yes." Lucy's pretty face lit up like the sun. She turned and hugged her mother, then put her head on Truth's knee and began to weep.

"Thee will have time for that later," said her mother. "I'll go to the barn and tell thy father to saddle one of the grays for thee." She hurried away.

"What shall I take?" Lucy asked Truth.

"Nothing except thy clothing, I would guess. He asked only for thee. He's in a cave."

"Cave?"

"Yes, I didn't know there was a cave on the Bardwell land till last night."

"How is Todd hurt?"

"He had a bullet in his leg, but a Virginia doctor took it out. He can't walk very well yet. Aunt Elizabeth is tending to him." Truth hesitated before saying, "Robert was with him at the battle. He does not know what happened to him. He lost sight of him in the smoke."

"Does he think Robert was killed?"

"No. No one found his body after the battle."

"Can't the Bardwells ask about him? Would the army tell them?"

"I don't know." Truth looked up. Friend Coxey, a portly, redheaded man, was coming toward them at a run, leading a leggy gray horse with saddle and bridle.

Without waiting to pack any clothing, Lucy got up into the saddle. She reined the gray around and started off at a canter. It wasn't necessary to nudge Hosea. The bay started off at a quick pace to catch up, and then Truth and Lucy rode together in silence until they reached the Bardwell farm.

Matthew Bardwell met them and lifted Lucy and Truth down. He ordered Truth, "Take Lucy to Todd. Tell thy aunt to come to the house. She needs the rest." He smiled at Lucy. "We are happy to see thee here. Thee will be the best medicine of all for Todd."

Lucy, who was weeping, flung her arms around her father-in-law. Then she asked Truth, "Take me to my husband now and leave me alone with him. If I need anything, I'll come to the house for it."

Leaving the horses to be led away by her uncle, Truth set out for the pasture and the great boulders with Lucy beside her. When they reached the cleft, Truth pulled back the thicket of greenery and said, "He's in there. Uncle Matthew says that's where he's got to stay because the army will come hunting him as a deserter."

Lucy nodded. "He'll get well, and then he can come out in the nighttime."

A week later, six Confederate cavalrymen came riding up to the Bardwell farm. To Truth's horror, one of the officers was the slave catcher Daniel Fields, looking most gallant in the South's elegant gray uniform. Hearing the jingle of their bridles, the older Bardwells came out of the house with Truth behind them.

Fields spoke first. "So, we meet again. This time we're hunting for two Quaker deserters by the names of Todd Bardwell and Robert Bardwell."

Truth touched her aunt's rigid arm. If the army thought Robert had deserted, then he had not been killed or wounded!

Matthew Bardwell answered him, saying, "Thee knows this farm. Thee has searched here before. Search again. Thee will find no runaway slaves and no deserters.''

"We plan to search, Quaker."

"When did you see your sons last?" demanded another officer.

"In May, when they left here to go north," answered Truth's uncle evenly.

"To fight for the Yankees?" asked the officer bitterly.

"No, not to fight at all but to make their way to Canada."

"That's the Quaker way, Jed," said Daniel Fields as he dismounted. "Nonetheless, you might be interested to know your sons were at the battle of Manassas."

"Were they?" asked Elizabeth Bardwell calmly.

"Yes, that's where they turned up missing."

The second officer added, "But a direct hit from a cannonball doesn't leave much of anything of a man to find."

"May God protect them and all others in battles!" said Truth's aunt as she turned away, walked to the front door, and held it open for the men to search the house.

As Daniel Fields brushed past Truth, she turned her back on him and whispered under her breath, "Look to your heart's content, slave catcher." She knew he wouldn't find the secret of the big hearthstone or the huge rocks in the pasture.

CHAPTER 8

Some News!

THE REMAINING MONTHS of 1861 passed slowly, with no news of Robert and with Todd a prisoner of sorts. But at least no more deserter hunters came searching for them.

The autumn reaping, corn shucking, and hog killing were done with the help of Quaker neighbors. In turn, Uncle Matthew did the same for them when they called for his aid. It was hard for them without the younger men. All had gone away or been forced into the army.

Though she was officially out of school now because of her age, Truth still attended; so did Martha. They were helpers to Mr. Hartling. He had asked them to stay on, saying he lived on borrowed time until he was forced into the Confederate army. Once he left, Truth and Martha would continue teaching the younger children.

Lucy came and went at the Bardwells' house, so her continued absence would not be noticed by the staunch southern patriots in Bentonville. When she was there, she stayed with Todd. Some evenings Todd would limp over to dine with his family, but he always returned to the Rocks to sleep, even though it was cold in winter and there was no way to warm the cave by fire without a telltale smoke outlet.

The new year brought few changes in the Bardwells' lives. The war had now come to North Carolina. Although the Confederacy lost Roanoke Island and Union bases were set up on forts Clark and Hatteras on the Atlantic, the Yankees did not overrun the state. News of battles elsewhere arrived in the spring when the weather improved and roads were passable. In April, the bloody battle of Shiloh in Tennessee and Mississippi was won by the Union. There was fighting in June in Virginia, and in late August a second battle—and Southern victory—at Manassas Junction. September saw more fighting in Maryland at Sharpsburg, a battle neither side won.

In October, Matthew Bardwell brought home

news from Goldsboro of the death of one of the tall Gibson sons, Lockwood, at the Maryland battle and the severe wounding of Daniel Fields. Coming into the kitchen upon his return, he told the women, "The man who told me said that Fields lost a leg." He sighed. "Losing a leg will put an end to his slave catching. But I take no pleasure in that, even though he treated Squire wickedly, or in the Gibson lad's death." He said to Aunt Elizabeth now, "I heard in Goldsboro that the draft age has been raised. They will be taking men from thirty-five to forty-five for the army come November. I am forty-four. I will have to pay five hundred dollars to stay out of the army. Thee knows what that will mean. We have spoken of it before."

Truth said, "Uncle, I never told thee, but I have some gold pieces Papa gave me. If thee needs them, I'll give them to thee."

He smiled. "Thank thee, child. Thee is a good daughter. Perhaps someday we may call on thee for it."

Aunt Elizabeth also smiled at Truth and then said, "Yes, husband, thee will have to sell the horses." Her husband nodded somberly. "And sell them to Confederates, too," he added with a sigh. "They're broke to the saddle. Before long they'll be cavalry mounts." He sighed again. "Our horses must go to the war, it seems. They'll have short lives. I'll take them to the horse market next week and will keep only the old plowhorse. He can pull the wagon and reaper."

Elizabeth Bardwell told him, "It would be better to sell them than have the Confederates come here and take them from us. Will they fetch five hundred dollars?"

"Yes, but not much more."

The woman shook her head. "Robert loved the horses best of all. Oh, where is he? Where is he? It's been so long."

Truth watched as her aunt put her hands to her face and left the room. She hastily said to her uncle, "Todd thinks Robert's alive, too."

"So do I."

"Todd says he'd know it in his heart if he wasn't."

"Yes, they were very close as children. I do believe that."

Sullen-skied November came in with cold blasts of wind that buffeted Truth's face as she went to school in the mornings. The fierceness matched her mood as it nipped her cheeks to a fiery pink.

Her uncle had sold the horses but had not received enough money to cover what he must pay. He'd had to drive some steers with the horses to the army buyers in Goldsboro. As Truth stood at the fence by Todd's hiding place and watched Matthew Bardwell leave, she had wiped tears from her face with her sleeve. She knew every horse and steer by name. She remembered what he'd said about horses dying in war, and it pained her. The steers she'd known as calves would be slaughtered for soldiers' meat.

Not only were cattle and horses being gathered for the renewal of the war next spring, men were gathered, too. Toward the end of the month, a Confederate sergeant and three soldiers in gray came to the schoolhouse to take Michael Hartling away with them. He hadn't tried to escape. He couldn't pay five hundred dollars and had expected the army to come after him. It did.

He said farewell to the children; then he asked to speak privately with Truth and Martha.

The sergeant scoffed, "Go ahead. Kiss your little girlies good-bye. We won't look."

Without a word, Michael Hartling led the girls around the corner of the schoolhouse. He told them, "I'm sorry about that. Keep the school going. You can do it. Remember, slaves can be hidden in the school loft, too."

Martha answered, "We know that. We'll sure try to keep the school. Good luck to thee, Mr. Hartling. I will not forget thee."

With tears running down her cheeks, Truth said to him, "I will keep thee in my prayers. Write to the school if thee can." She looked hard at him. He was going away and, like Robert, might never come back. Truth realized that she had deeper feelings for him than she'd guessed.

He didn't touch Martha, but he pulled Truth to him and held her to his side for an instant. Then he hurried back to where the soldiers waited.

Martha said, "He cares for thee, Truth."

Truth nodded. "As thee cares for Robert."

The war came very close to the Bardwells in the freezing cold days of early December. Federal troops fought Confederates at the Neuse River and in the woods that lay about it. Would the Union take Goldsboro or the river? No, they failed, and Goldsboro remained in southern hands.

It took almost a month—until the very end of January 1863—for the great news of the Emancipation Proclamation to reach North Carolina. On January 1, this decree issued by President Lincoln had abolished slavery in the Rebel states. Martha had read it in a newspaper and announced it to the children at the school. Almost all of them scoffed at its foolishness except for the Quakers, who had to rejoice in secret.

There was another secret at that time, too, that only Martha and Truth could share. Two nights before the welcome news of the proclamation had arrived, a young female runaway slave had come to the Bardwell farm. A house servant, she'd heard of the president's decree and decided now was the time to flee from her South Carolina masters.

Truth had sat beside her in the wagon in broad daylight. Both wore deep black silk bonnets, dark dresses, and heavy shawls and mittens. They appeared to be two Quaker girls on their way somewhere. How Truth's heart pounded as Uncle Matthew pulled the wagon over to the side of the road and waited as soldiers in Confederate gray, two units of cavalry and one marching infantry, passed by, heading north. No one questioned them.

The war went on and on. Matthew Bardwell went less often to Goldsboro. There was little to buy there—no sugar, coffee, or white flour. Honey was used as a sweetener. Bitter-tasting weeds were dried for coffee. Home-ground cornmeal became their only flour.

No news of the war came until May, and then it was disheartening. A Confederate general named Robert E. Lee had won battles in Virginia. Truth wondered if Robert had been there.

The blazing hot July of 1863 brought more news; this time it was startling. General Lee took the war to the northern states! He'd marched his army up through Virginia and Maryland into Pennsylvania. At a little town there called Gettysburg, the Confederates met the forces of Union general George Meade and fought a terrible three-day battle in fierce heat.

Lucy brought the news in an old newspaper from her father. It was ten days old. The paper said not only that the battle of Gettysburg had been a dreadful and costly fight, but also that Lee had retreated to Virginia and the Union forces had taken the city of Vicksburg on the Mississippi River.

"Where is Robert during all this?" cried Elizabeth Bardwell. "Will we never hear? He's been lost to us for two whole years. He must be dead!"

"Todd says no," insisted her husband.

"But why don't we hear?"

Truth murmured, "We don't hear from Mr. Hartling, either. I think that letters written to Quakers are not delivered to them."

"That is probably the truth," agreed her uncle.

News of Robert Bardwell finally came at the sultry end of August, and from a most unexpected source. One afternoon, Perry Gibson came riding bareback on a mule up to the house while Truth listlessly hung laundry on the clothesline in the yard. Perry had left school to work on his father's farm and she'd seen him only a few times since. After his brother Lockwood's death, he'd been more quiet in his behavior. He was thin and ragged, and his mule's ribs showed.

Perry reined in next to Truth and said, "I've brought you news. My oldest brother, Ward, got sent home by the army the other day. He was in that big scrap up in Pennsylvania. He's wounded bad in the shoulder, so he can't fight no more."

Truth waited, a clothespin still in her mouth. Would Perry taunt her? It was clear that he had something more to say.

He went on, "It's about your cousin Robert."

The pin fell to the ground as Truth stared and then said hurriedly, "Wait till I go get my aunt and uncle."

"No, I don't want to talk with them, but I'll tell you. My brother said Robert and Todd never turned into soldiers the way our officers wanted. They got put out front in that first battle at Manassas. Robert came through it, and some soldiers marched him off with them after it was over. But Ward says they never did find hide nor hair of Todd."

"We fear he's dead," lied Truth. "Soldiers came here hunting for him. They said he disappeared on the battlefield at Manassas and could have been hit by a cannonball. They said they didn't know anything about Robert."

Perry lifted his hand and scratched his head.

95

"Ward don't know about Todd, neither, but he reckons that Robert was marched away real fast before he got a chance to run away to the Yankees." He suddenly nodded. "Well, that might not have been such a good notion after all, if he ever had it in mind. Ward saw Robert at Gettysburg. He was out in front the way he'd been at the other fight. My brother saw what happened to him there."

Truth sucked in her breath and waited.

Perry continued, "Just before Ward got hit in the shoulder, he saw a big Yankee soldier grab hold of Robert, whirl him around, and march him away at the end of a bayonet."

"What?"

"That's what he says. The last he saw of Robert was when that Yankee was prodding him in the back with a bayonet. A bayonet's a knife at the end of a rifle. Know what that means?"

"No, what?" Even though she asked, Truth wasn't sure she wanted to know.

"We think it means your cousin Robert is a prisoner of the Yankees. They took him prisoner just as if he'd been a real soldier for the South. Ain't that something, though?"

A prisoner of the *North?* Truth's head spun. So Perry wouldn't see her pain, she bent down for the clothespin, picked it up, and looked at it, turning it in her fingers. Robert had whittled it for his mother. He was a fine whittler, better than Todd. She asked, "Where would the Yankees take him, Perry?"

"I don't know. Some jail somewhere up north. They got them for southern prisoners just like we do for Yankees. There's one in Charleston called Castle Pinckney."

Truth said, "I thank thee, Perry." She looked into his face. No, there was no glitter of satisfaction in his blue eyes. She asked, "Why did thee bring me this news?"

Perry sighed. "I don't know, Truth. I reckon with Lockwood dead and Ward wounded so bad there ain't so much pleasure in war no more. All I want is for us to win it and get it over with. I wish I was back at school, not just doing farmwork and fetching and carrying for my sick brother and my pa, who feels poorly, too. My brother said in his way Robert was brave. He'd never take up a rifle even though they done real bad things to him in camp to break his spirit. It's strange, but he never got one scratch on him anytime he was in battle. We hadn't expected Quakers to be brave."

Truth nodded. She said, "Friends can be very strong and brave. We have to be."

"I reckon so. You sure got pretty hair." Astonishingly, Perry lifted his straw hat to her like a gentleman, put it back on, and reined the mule away to go home.

Truth waited until he was out of sight, and then ran to the house, slamming the back door behind her.

She found her aunt and Lucy scalding the milk churn in the kitchen, getting ready to churn butter. Half-laughing, half-crying, Truth ran first to her aunt and hugged her, then to Todd's pretty wife.

"What is it, child? What's happened?" asked Aunt Elizabeth.

"It's Robert. He's alive! He's alive! He was in battles, but he never got hurt one bit. Perry Gibson brought me the news just now. Robert's alive. His brother Ward saw Robert at Gettysburg."

Lucy was the first to speak after hearing the amazing news. "Where is he now?" she asked, as she set the kettle back on the stove.

"Perry says Ward thinks Robert's in one of the Yankee prisons."

"Prison?" cried Elizabeth Bardwell, whose expression had gone from joy to horror. "Prison? Go fetch thy uncle from the barn, Truth." She sighed. "This may not be so good a piece of news as we think. Prisons are evil places. We Friends have had much experience with prisons, both as prisoners and as workers with prisoners. Pray to heaven the one where Robert is is not a bad one. Did Perry give thee any news as to where it is?"

"He didn't know."

Her aunt shook her head. "Bring thy uncle here, Truth, and thee, Lucy, run and tell Todd. His prison here with us is a gentle one to bear because we love him. Robert's may not be."

Truth flew to the barn where her uncle was bent over, treating a spring-born heifer with a split hoof. Breathlessly, Truth told him, "Uncle, Perry Gibson fetched us news of Robert. He's alive. Perry's brother saw him at the battle of Gettysburg. He wouldn't fight. The Gibsons think he's in a Yankee prison."

Matthew Bardwell straightened up at once. "Where is it, child? Did he tell thee?"

"He said he didn't know."

Her uncle's face darkened. "There could be several places for prisoners of the war in the North. Yes, if the Yankees found him among Rebel soldiers in a battle, they'd take him prisoner. If he said he was a Friend and would not fight for the South, they'd try to force him to fight for them. When he wouldn't fight at all, they'd keep him a prisoner."

"It isn't fair!" wailed Truth.

"Many things in life are not."

"Aunt Elizabeth wants to see thee right now."

"Yes, of course, I'll come."

"What shall we do?" asked the girl.

Her uncle frowned, knitting his dark brows. After a pause, he said, "We Friends are known to work in jails and prisons wherever they are. Friends in the North could find Robert!"

"How could they do that? We can't write letters to the North."

"No, but messages can travel on the Underground Railroad as well as slaves, and more easily. Our first step will be to take a message to Friend Buchan."

Truth clasped her hands with hope. Why hadn't she thought of that? She asked, "Would thee take me with thee?"

"Yes, child, that is a good idea. If we're stopped, I'll say I am taking thee to the doctor in Goldsboro."

"When shall we go?"

"Tonight—as soon as the moon rises. With so many soldiers about, I don't want to take the wagon and lanterns out on the road to attract their attention."

The rest of the day dragged by for Truth. Finally, as the moon rose, she and her uncle set out on the plowhorse, with Truth seated behind him. They took the road north and rode slowly. No one challenged them along the way, so Truth did not have to pretend to cough even once.

They arrived at the Buchans' house near midnight and awakened the farmer, who came out in his nightshirt. William Buchan asked, "I see Truth with thee. Thee has no slave for me, Friend Bardwell?"

"Not this time. I have a message—"

Truth burst in, "May I see Martha, please?"

"She is in her bed. Go up to her. Thee knows the way," said Friend Buchan.

Sliding off the horse while the men spoke, Truth ran into the house to Martha's room. She rapped on the door and heard Martha's mumbled "Who's that?" She answered, "Truth," and hurried in.

Moonlight fell on her friend's face as she sat

up. Truth perched on the side of the bed, took hold of one of Martha's hands, and said, "Perry Gibson brought me news today. He told me Robert is alive!"

"Alive?"

"Yes," answered Truth, and quickly told Martha the news. She ended by saying, "We're sending a message on the railroad to find out where Robert is being held. It won't be written down on paper. All it will be is something like, 'Where is Robert Bardwell, a young Friend from near Goldsboro, North Carolina, who was forced into the Confederate army and captured by Union soldiers at Gettysburg?' It's to go to Friends in the North. If they find out, they'll send a message the same way down here to us."

"Oh, Truth, what if they made him go into the Union army?"

"He won't fight for them, either, Martha."

CHAPTER 9

From the North and to It

AFTER EVERY FIRST Day meeting, the Bardwells spoke with other Friends, gathering whatever news they could. In windy October, they
heard of a mid-September Union victory in
Tennessee, and in December of another one in
that same state. News traveled even more slowly
now because the Quakers spoke little with the
townspeople, who spat and cursed at them.
Yankee victories were hateful, and the Quakers
were a handy target for the southerners' anger.

The New Year of 1864 came in grimly, with
still no news about Robert. Truth and Martha
went on teaching at the little school, and twice
Lydia brought letters Michael Hartling had sent
to her family and shared them with her friends.

He was working in an army hospital as a male nurse, not as a soldier. His father was a doctor, and he knew enough medicine to be chosen for that kind of job.

When Truth told Todd this news, he nodded and said, "He won't be going into any battles then. The nurses stay back of the lines. That makes thee happy, doesn't it? I bet thee likes him better than thee has ever said."

Truth felt a red flush creep up from her neck, which made Todd and Lucy laugh. It was good to hear Todd laugh. He was well by now and hated being cooped up.

Finally, long months after the Bardwells' message had been sent north, the railroad brought word of him. Friend Buchan brought it early on a sultry Saturday morning in August. Martha rode beside her father in the rickety wagon pulled by their old white mare. Their horses, cows, and better wagon had been taken by the southern government. They had been paid in Confederate money that was worth little, but then, what was there to buy?

Truth, her aunt, and Lucy hiked up their skirts and ran to the wagon with Uncle Matthew lumbering behind.

"Is it news of Robert?" cried his mother.

"It is." Friend Buchan leaned down. "We have located him, Sister. The message came at dawn from a stranger who was passing through. All he said was, 'Friend Robert Bardwell is at the new Federal prison in Elmira, New York.'"

"New York?" cried Truth. "That's so far away from here!"

"It is," agreed Martha's father. He asked the Bardwells, "Will thee tell the news tomorrow at the meeting?"

Truth looked at her uncle and saw him frown and tug at his lower lip. "No, but I shall ask advice of the elders. Now that we know where Robert is, matters have changed."

The other man shook his head. "We cannot trust the message for certain."

"We know that."

After the meeting, Truth waited with her aunt, Lucy, and Lucy's family, watching Matthew Bardwell talk with three old men beside the log house. The women waited for a long time. At last, the men shook hands, nodded solemnly, and went to their wagons.

As Matthew Bardwell got up onto the seat and gathered up the reins, his look was grim. He turned to his wife and said, "Elder Shaw says that he read in a Virginia newspaper that army prisoners who are Friends have been set free by petition from President Lincoln. They think, and I think, that I should go to Elmira and see for myself if Robert is truly there."

"How can thee do that?" asked Elizabeth Bardwell with a catch in her voice.

His voice was grating, as he replied, "The same way Squire and Liley and the slaves got to the North. I cannot hope to get a travel pass from the officials in Goldsboro. Where the slaves were hidden, I can be hidden, too. I can come home as Todd did."

"Husband, thy speech is that of a man from North Carolina. That could make great trouble for thee in the North. They'll take thee for a Confederate."

"No, I shall not go alone, and I shall not speak once I am in the North. Someone else can do that for me."

"Who could that be?"

Listening in the back of the wagon, Truth felt a quick surge of excitement in her chest, as if yeast were rising there. She squirmed around to touch her aunt on the shoulder and said, "I talk like folks in Indiana. Everybody here tells me that. That's a Yankee state."

"Truth?" Her aunt stared at her.

"Yes, nobody would take me for a southerner, because I'm not."

"Does thee mean to take Truth?" asked Aunt Elizabeth.

Her uncle nodded. "Yes, there is no one else who will do. In the North, she will say that she is my niece and I am a mute. We'll dress as Friends, peaceful people. Elder Shaw said the newspaper reported that prisoners die like flies in army prisons. There is much sickness and overcrowding in these places, and the food is poor. I must get to Elmira to see if our son is truly in prison and still alive. Then I shall travel to Washington to see Mr. Lincoln."

"Mr. Lincoln," marveled Lucy, speaking for the first time.

Matthew Bardwell went on to his wife, "What few crops I planted this year of oats and corn must be harvested. The elders will send men to help thee while we are away. At all costs, Todd must stay hidden. Thee and Lucy must operate our station." He turned around to look at Truth, his face shadowed by his broad-brimmed hat. He asked her quietly, "Will thee go with me, child? We should go soon—tonight."

Choosing her words carefully, Truth told him earnestly, "If thee had not asked me, I would have followed thee to Friend Buchan's when thee left, and followed thee when thee left for the next station. Thee and thy wife took me in as a daughter and have been kind to me. I know thee has little money anymore, but I have some." Now her speech quickened. "When we get to the North, we shall ride on a real railroad to Elmira. Maybe we shall get to see New York City as well as Washington."

Elizabeth Bardwell looked shocked. She scolded, "Truth! Daughter! This will not be a hayride. Thee may hide in terrible places thee cannot imagine. Husband, is this right?"

"Is Robert dying in prison right?"

Lucy had the final word. "I'd go—I'd leave Todd if I could fill Truth's shoes in this. Thee must try to rescue his brother."

"Thank thee, Lucy," whispered Truth as she sat back, thinking. The glow she had felt when she volunteered enveloped her once more. What a very good opinion of her and Indiana the elders had. Truth hadn't thought they even noticed her, but they surely had. There must have been much talk about the Bardwells' Indiana kettle cousin and her part in the Underground Railroad.

Her uncle added to the glow when he remarked, "Elder Shaw says that Truth has a solid and godly spirit, quick wits, and a nimble tongue. Friend Dunn praised her also."

The radiance turned a soft golden yellow, and Truth shivered. Going north, going tonight. The first stop would be at the Buchans'. Where would the others be?

After the farewell supper at which Todd joined them, there were tears and long embraces. Just after dark, Matthew Bardwell and his niece left on horseback for the Buchans' house. They took one small carpetbag with them and nothing more. Though the August night was hot, they wore heavy underclothing they might need later. Deeply engrossed in thoughts of the dangers they were to face, the travelers kept to their own counsel.

William Buchan, his wife, and Martha were stunned to hear of their real errand when Matthew Bardwell told them, "This time, Truth and I are the contraband. We ask to be taken on to the next station north. We're on our way to New York, to Elmira."

Martha asked breathlessly, her plain face shining, "Thee are going after him?"

"Yes, the elders believe President Lincoln will help a Quaker get out of prison. Truth has a northern voice. She will speak for me."

"Truth, thee goes, too?" Martha said in amazement.

Truth nodded. "If we can, we'll bring him home."

While Martha's eyes filled with tears, her father said, "I'll take thee to the next station. Do not be surprised that thee will be blindfolded so thee will not know the place again from the outside. This is not necessary with slaves, who travel only one way. Thee will see only one person, an old man. He is not a Friend, but he is against slavery. He will send thee on as swiftly as he can."

"And my horse?" asked Uncle Matthew.

"I shall take it back to Sister Bardwell tomorrow. Martha shall ride it alongside my wagon. I'll put thee in the false bottom of my wagon. It will be dark and hot in there, and the ride will jolt thee even though I have spread out some blankets. Make no noise till I halt and strike the wagon three times to let thee know we have arrived. Then I shall leave thee at once at Station Eight. Give me thy hand, Friend Bardwell. May our God protect thee and give thee thy desire."

As the two Quaker men clasped hands, Sister Buchan and then Martha embraced Truth. Martha whispered in her ear, "Oh, please, Truth, fetch Robert home. I want the three of thee to come back on our railroad."

Truth soon crept into the hiding place in the Buchan wagon after her uncle. The space was musty-smelling and airless, but she found she wasn't too cramped. The blankets helped a little to ease the hardness under her spine.

"Have courage, Truth," came her uncle's whisper.

Then the wagon started off with a jolt, and Truth slid from front to back.

Sleepless hours passed until finally Truth felt the wagon stop and heard the triple rap on its side. The bottom was opened, and she and her uncle crawled out to find William Buchan and a gray-bearded old man with a lantern standing beside the wagon.

"Blindfold them—then be on your way," ordered the old man, and Friend Buchan did, using cotton scarves.

Truth heard the wagon leaving and felt panic until the old man said, "Take my hand, girl, when I grab yours. And, mister, I'm going to put yours on her head. I'll lead you. After you eat a little meat and some water and corn bread, I'll take you to the next station. If you smell turnips, it's 'cause you're going into my root cellar. Leave them blindfolds on."

"We thank thee, friend," murmured Matthew Bardwell. "How many stations will take us to the North?"

"I don't know. Maybe five more. That's my guess."

After a little food and a visit to a privy, Truth and her uncle were taken to a wagon. Their blindfolds were removed only after they were secreted under a bundle of dusty turnip sacks. Their trip was a long and thirsty one, despite the bottle of water the old man had given them. They heard the noises of other wagon wheels, dogs barking, and hoarse voices.

At last, the old man halted the wagon and shook the sacks, saying, "We're here. Come on out. The boy'll take you from now on. Good luck to you whatever you're up to, even if it ain't any of my business. Put your blindfolds back on and wait by the road."

Helped by her uncle, Truth got stiffly out of the old man's wagon and looked about at the empty countryside. She put on the blindfold again and stood waiting in the dusk. Soon she heard the old man leave after whistling twice. No whistle answered his.

The Quakers waited for a time and then Truth heard running footsteps and a young voice. "Come, take my hand and my sister's hand. We'll take thee to the privy, then to where thee should go."

Friends? Truth thought they were—the "thee" had given them away. Her spirits rose.

This time they went inside a house that smelled of freshly baked bread. Doors opened and shut behind them as they went upstairs, walking hand in hand with the unseen children. There was a creaking noise, and then they were helped into what seemed to be a small space.

"It is a secret room," whispered Truth's uncle.

Before long, food came—ham and peas, potatoes and gravy—as well as warm water, soap, and towels. All were delivered by unseen people. When they had finished eating, the two of them were led to cots to rest comfortably.

Truth asked, "Can thee tell me if we are still in North Carolina?"

"No, we cannot," came a woman's voice. Her tone changed to one of suspicion as she said, "Thee has a northern voice. Why is that?"

Matthew Bardwell answered, "She was reared in Indiana and is my sister's daughter. My sister was born in North Carolina."

"Oh, that explains thy accent. Rest while thee may. Then we'll go on in the morning."

Suddenly, Truth heard a child giggle and say, "It's well they don't see what they ride in, Mama. They might not like a hearse."

"Be still, child. The hearse is useful. No one searches it."

The next day's journey was not too unpleasant, though it was made in a most strange equipage. Truth and her uncle rode in the hearse a long way and at last stopped in what sounded like a barnyard. No dogs barked, although hogs grunted.

Once again blindfolded, they heard only a man's deep voice as he took them into his hog-scented barn and said, "Get under the floorboards. I'll guide thee down. Then I'll set the boards back in place and pitch hay over them. Thee will find food and water there. I'll take thee on at midnight in my buggy."

Oh, what a strange ride that was—mile after blindfolded mile down rutted roads that jerked the travelers about in the rickety, springless buggy. The driver turned to the left, to the right, to the left again, then to the right. Dogs barked at the buggy as it passed in the night.

Truth heard nary a human voice until the driver ordered, "Take off thy blindfolds when I leave thee." He laughed. "We are over the Virginia border and in Maryland. Welcome to the North. Thee are fortunate. There were few Confederate cavalrymen out and about tonight to ask if thee have papers. Walk a mile north till thee see a white farmhouse with two chimneys. Friends there will greet thee. I do not know what takes thee on this desperate journey, but it must mean very much to thee. I wish thee the blessings of our faith."

"Thank thee, good Friend," answered Matthew Bardwell. "We have come to get my son out of a Union army prison."

"Then thee will need all the blessings, Friend."

* * *

How good it was to stretch their legs after so much confinement, Truth thought. The night was warm and dark, and so peaceful it was hard to believe there was a war raging and more fighting to come. Would it never end?

The white farmhouse soon loomed ahead on the left side of the road. Someone was awake inside, for a kerosene lamp sat in one of the downstairs windows. Trusting to the words of their last conductor, Uncle Matthew and Truth went directly to the door and softly knocked.

The door was opened by a tall young woman. Her dress indicated that she was a Quaker. She had taken the lamp and now held it up to show her the callers. The woman looked, then asked, "I am Rhoda Quisenbery. Is thee Friend Bard-well?"

"I am," he said, surprised at her question.

"Get thee inside. We have been expecting thee since we answered thy message about thy son."

"It came through here?" marveled the man as he and Truth entered a handsomely furnished parlor.

"It did, indeed," came an old man's voice

116

from a deep chair. The man got up to shake Matthew Bardwell's hand. Truth saw that he was tall. "I am Friend Quisenbery. I went to the telegraph office in Hagerstown and sent a message asking about a Robert Bardwell. The prison warden in Elmira said thy son is indeed a prisoner. A few days ago I sent another, and got a reply that he is still there."

"I must see him with my own eyes," said Truth's uncle.

"Yes, thee should, Friend. But now come eat a cold supper and take to thy beds."

Rhoda Quisenbery asked, "In the morning, would thee like to bathe and have thy clothing washed?"

"Oh, yes, I would," cried Truth, looking at her dirty dress and boots.

"Thee has a northern voice!" exclaimed the woman.

Uncle Matthew explained once more, "She is my niece who comes from Indiana. We thought Truth would speak for me in the North. I cannot be taken for a spy."

"That is wise," agreed the old Quaker. "Tomorrow afternoon we shall take thee to town and put thee on the train to New York City. From there, thee will take another to Elmira."

"Will it be that easy?" breathed Matthew Bardwell.

"If all goes well, it could be. What does thee plan to do about thy son?"

"After we have seen him, we will go to Washington, tell President Lincoln his story, and ask that he order Robert's release. We'll take the letter to Elmira, and then we'll go home again."

"Oh, thee has great expectations," cried the woman.

"Or great faith," added the old man.

"We have great faith—and great love, Truth and I."

"We will pray for thy success. Now come— eat and rest."

What a fine collection of baked meats, fowl, white bread, cheese, and garden vegetables, thought Truth as she ate her fill. The Bardwells had not had such food for two full years. Her bed was so soft and deep that she fell onto it only half-undressed. She slept so heavily that Sister Quisenbery had to shake her awake.

"It's ten o'clock, my dear. Thy uncle has bathed and gone to town with my grandfather to buy train tickets. I've heated the water for thee in the kitchen, and while thee soaks, I will tend to thy clothing as best I can."

"Thank thee, thank thee" was all that Truth could say. Oh, to smell soap and feel warm water again!

By two o'clock, Truth and her uncle were seated in a railroad car behind the black steam locomotive, waiting in the Hagerstown station to travel north. Side by side on soot-stained red plush seats, they looked out the window at the platform where blue-clad Union soldiers either lounged or walked about, talking and exercising. More soldiers sat in their very car just across the aisle, ahead of and behind them.

One soldier, a big man with bushy blond side-whiskers and an arrogant manner, now asked to see their passes for civilian travel. Friend Quisenbery had been able to obtain passes for them by telling the authorities in Hagerstown that Matthew Bardwell and Truth were Indiana Quakers on their way to New York City. They were supposedly going there to consult a doctor in hopes of finding a cure for his inability to speak since he'd had a seizure in the spring. Friend Quisenbery had said that they'd seen a

Maryland doctor and were being sent north by him. Truth traveled with her uncle as his spokesperson.

Truth now showed the soldier their passes as she had shown them earlier to the train conductor. The man examined them, shook his head, handed them back, and told her, "Thank you, missy. I hope your uncle finds a doctor who can do him some good."

Truth said, "We hope so. We've come a long way from Indiana."

"What part of it? I'm from Indiana myself. Just hearing you talk makes me feel homesick. Have you ever been on a train before?"

Truth told him the name of her village and said, "No, sir, we got here by wagon." She dared to ask, "Will there be another battle soon?"

"More than likely. And more than likely in Virginia again. Us soldiers sort of mill around and get sent here and there. When a Johnny Reb army runs smack dab into us or some Confederate or Union general decides it's time to fight, we fight."

"Was thee at Gettysburg?"

"There, and at other places."

"When will the war be over?"

"When one side gives up—that'll be the only way. Sit back now and try not to get sick from all the cigar smoke. If you do, open the window and throw up. Lots of folks do that. Don't be ashamed."

"I thank thee."

Truth thought she had best stop talking before she said too much. She was relieved when the train whistle suddenly shrieked and the iron wheels beneath them began to turn.

They were on their way to rescue Robert!

CHAPTER 10

An Old Friend and Some New Ones

THEY ARRIVED AT the end of their slow journey a day later. Truth had slept very little on the train but still had the strength and curiosity to stare out her window at the great city she had heard so much about. New York City seemed great indeed. The train went by miles of brick buildings, most of them three and four stories tall.

Finally, the train stopped, letting out a last, great puff of steam. The enormous station was filled with people—prosperous-looking men in tall hats and fine frock coats, and women splendid in wide crinoline skirts of bright summer colors. Their little bonnets were covered with feathers, lace, and artificial flowers that looked so real Truth could scarcely believe they were not real roses and violets. She saw not one black, scuttle-shaped Quaker bonnet among them. Soldiers walked about, too, going and coming down the various tracks to and from trains. Never had she seen so large a crowd. It frightened her.

Her uncle nudged her and nodded as he pointed to the crowd. Yes, they must get off, and she must ask at a ticket window for the next train to Elmira. She got down from the train and he followed, carrying their carpetbag as they walked into the throng.

And then it happened! There was a shriek from a woman and a sudden movement in the crowd, a swift parting, that left the two Quakers standing alone. Truth looked ahead and saw a mob of men and boys in plug hats and shabby clothes surge toward them at a run. Some brandished sticks like weapons. The big, red-faced man who led them yelled to the others, "We found us one, boys! A Quaker, a no-good Quaker who won't go fight for Abe Lincoln or nobody else. See them, lads?"

Stunned, Truth stood beside her uncle but was knocked aside into the shouting crowd. She saw Uncle Matthew fall down under a barrage of fists and feet. She tried to cry out for help, but a hand came out of nowhere to cover her mouth. A moment later, she was jerked off her feet and away from the mob as whistles began to blow.

Struggling as hard as she could, trying to bite the hand and kick backward, Truth was hauled away. When her captor felt he was far enough away from the mob, he shook her and said quietly, "You know me. It's Squire. Stop fighting me." He let go.

Truth whirled around to see the former slave the Bardwells had sent north twice on the Underground Railroad. He stood before her, strong, tall, and well-dressed.

"Squire! Please help my uncle."

"The police are there. Hear the whistles? What can I do against twenty? Friend Quisenbery sent me word that you and your uncle were coming here, so I came to meet you."

"We came to get Robert out of Elmira prison."

Squire gave Truth a surprised look but said only, "Let's go look to Mr. Bardwell now."

The girl and man threaded their way through the gawking crowd to the place where Matthew Bardwell lay with a bloody forehead on the station floor. His attackers had fled, and police bent over him.

Squire asked one of them, "How is he?"

"Bad hurt, I'm afraid."

"Oh, no!" wailed Truth.

"Do you know this Quaker?" asked the policeman.

"He's my uncle."

Squire told him, "I am his friend. I'll see to it that he's taken to Quakers I know here. They'll tend to everything." Squire now took a small white card from his pocket and gave it to the policeman. "I work for this printer."

The New Yorker grunted. "I see it. I know your boss."

Squire turned to Truth. "Stay here with your uncle. I'll fetch some Friends I know. They'll bring a wagon."

"Thank you, I will." Weeping, Truth sat down, took her uncle's limp hand in hers, and held it to her cheek. They were so close to Elmira and now this horror! A policeman stayed with her but did not talk as she sat crying, thinking.

Three-quarters of an hour later, Squire and three men in Quaker dress strode up to her and looked down at her uncle. One of the black-clad men knelt beside Matthew Bardwell, feeling his pulse and lifting his eyelids. He finally said, "He's unconscious. This is a pity. He did not know that Friends do not go about alone in this city. Come, we'll take him to my house. He'll have proper care among us. I am Dr. Porter."

Truth said, "I thank thee." Then she asked, "May Squire come with us? I must talk more with him."

"Yes, of course. He says thee and thy uncle are on an important mission."

Truth got up now and wiped her eyes. "We are!" She took a deep breath. "I will try to carry it out—without my uncle."

"Thee—a child, a girl?"

"Yes." She turned to Squire. "Will thee help me?"

He nodded. "I will, but we will need someone else's help, too. We'll go to Washington to see abolition's great friend. His name is Frederick Douglass. I think he will help you if he can."

"Thee knows Frederick Douglass?" asked one of the Quakers.

Squire nodded again. "I know the great abolitionist enough to know he's in Washington right now. Because he was once a slave himself, he may hear this girl."

Truth followed behind her uncle's unconscious body as he was carried out to a black wagon. After thanking the other Quakers as they left, she climbed up into the wagon with Squire and the doctor, and off they went. Because the wagon was closed on all sides, she saw nothing of the city—and she cared to see nothing as she sat on a bench beside her uncle, who lay on a litter on the floor.

As the wagon passed smoothly over paved streets, she asked Squire, "Would Mr. Douglass help us?"

"I hope so. He quarreled with the president over enlisting black soldiers in the Union army. He wanted that before Lincoln did. Finally, the president agreed, but Douglass says he should have done it earlier. Still, Frederick Douglass has powerful friends in Washington."

"I am happy to hear that," said the Quaker doctor. He asked Squire, "When will thee go?"

"Tomorrow morning."

Tears of weariness and frustration came to Truth's eyes once more as she told the doctor, "We haven't got much money. Nobody in the South has these days. I can pay my fare to Washington, but how can I pay thee thy fee?"

The doctor touched her hand. "Thee need

not pay. Go to Washington and have no fear for thy uncle. When he's well enough, we will send him home. Thee knows how!" Now he turned to Squire. "Thee had best not go alone with the girl."

Squire nodded in agreement. "No, my wife will be coming with us. And then we both plan to go to Liberia to live before the end of the year. We have our tickets. We want our children to be born in Africa. But first, we want to repay the Bardwells for what they did for us. I will never forget the two times the family helped me. I'll go to see Frederick Douglass and, if we're lucky, go to Elmira. This girl"—he looked at Truth—"this brave girl and her cousin Robert can go home then." He grinned. "You have said how, Doctor Porter."

The doctor smiled, then touched Truth's hand and said, "Thee must sleep at my house overnight in a good soft bed." He asked Squire, "When will thee come for her?"

"At seven in the morning. The train leaves at eight o'clock. I've taken it before. We'll be in Washington by the evening. I'll find out where Frederick Douglass stays. It will not be difficult." He frowned. "Reaching President Lincoln will be the difficult part."

* * *

Dr. Porter's brisk, black-haired wife fed Truth and showed her to a pleasant room. At six the next morning, she was awakened and allowed to visit her uncle, who still lay unconscious in bed with a bandaged head. She kissed him on the cheek and then left to eat her breakfast.

Squire was there at seven, as he had promised, and with him was his wife, Liley. She was slender and pretty, with delicate features and large, shining dark eyes. Her smile was warm as she held out her hands to Truth. "We hope to see Mr. Douglass tonight. Squire has sent him an overnight telegraph message so he'll know we are coming."

Truth turned to the doctor's wife and said, "I thank thee. I know thee and thy husband will care for my uncle and send him to us when thee can."

"Yes, dear. Thee can rely on us as Friends. Go now. God take care of thee and make smooth thy way."

Squire, Liley, and Truth left for the train station in a hired horse cab. They went down narrow streets filled with carts and carriages out so early in the day. How noisy and crowded this city was!

When they arrived at the station, they walked through the building, passing the spot where the hoodlums had attacked her uncle. Truth shuddered. During the ride, Liley had told her why Quakers were held in such contempt. There had been riots in New York City last summer over the first Federal draft call. There was much ill will toward blacks, who were considered the cause of the vicious war. Some had been killed, and an orphanage for black children had been burned. As a sect that aided many blacks to freedom, Quakers were hated. It was dangerous for them to go out at night.

Knowing this now, Truth looked anxiously about her, marking people's glances at the three of them. Mostly they were curious, but some were unfriendly. She was happy when they boarded the train. She felt safe there.

One thing could surely be said for Washington—it wasn't one bit like Goldsboro, North Carolina. Truth had expected it to be a larger Goldsboro. It wasn't!

This city didn't seem to be finished yet, with its big buildings set far enough apart so that a person had quite a walk to get from one to another. Some of the biggest ones had scaffolding around them, with cubes of gleaming white marble and large stones and pieces of timbers lying nearby.

Washington was humid and hot and smelled of a swamp. Swarms of gnats and mosquitoes bedeviled the three travelers and the horse and driver that Squire had hailed. Though it was early evening, the streets, muddy from a recent rain, were full of people. Most of the men she saw were blue-coated soldiers who constantly saluted one another as they stepped carefully around puddles and ruts. Trinket peddlers and oyster vendors accosted them. Hoop-skirted ladies walked in pairs under parasols.

Squire pointed out the buildings to her. "That one is the Capitol, the one with a dome being constructed. It'll have a statue of Freedom on top pretty soon."

"Where's President Lincoln?"

"At the Executive Mansion."

"Where's Mr. Douglass?"

"At the Kirkwood Hotel on Twelfth Street. Look there. See that big building with all the windows? That's the Willard Hotel."

Truth looked. The building was very large,

but it was not as interesting as the sight of a group of Confederate soldiers walking along under guard.

"Reb prisoners," said Squire, noticing her stare. "The men on the other side of the street—the ones in pale blue with crutches and canes—they're wounded Union soldiers. There are plenty of army hospitals in Washington."

"How long will we be here?" she asked, thinking of her gold coins. She sensed the money wouldn't go far.

Squire answered, "Not long if we're lucky. It all depends on Mr. Douglass."

The famous Frederick Douglass met the three of them in a little room off the red-and-gold lobby of the Kirkwood Hotel. Truth gaped at him as he shook hands with Squire. He was wonderfully handsome—a big, bronze-skinned man with strong features, gleaming dark eyes, a mane of black hair streaked with gray, and a full beard to match. He wore elegant black broadcloth.

Once he had greeted Squire and Liley, he turned to Truth and said in a deep and musical voice, "What can I do for you, Quaker maid? Take off your bonnet. I want to see your eyes."

Frightened, Truth obeyed and then fell silent. Only when nudged by Liley did she answer, "It's my cousin, Mr. Douglass. His name is Robert Bardwell, and he's in the Federal prison in Elmira. He didn't want to be a Confederate soldier." She rushed on and on, telling him about the Underground Railroad because she knew of his deep interest in it, and ended with, "My uncle's sick at a doctor's house in New York, and Squire brought me here to thee because perhaps thee could get the president to help me get Robert out."

Now Douglass spoke. "It is quite a story, child. Perhaps I can help you." He frowned. "But not through Mr. Lincoln. I think I know a better way. Sit down here and wait."

Squire, his wife, and Truth sat on fancy red plush chairs with thin gilded legs while Frederick Douglass went over to an ornate desk. He took a sheet of hotel stationery, wrote on it, and folded it. Handing the note to Truth, he said, "I have a liking for Quakers. Once I was a runaway slave, too. When I stood afraid beside a road, a Quaker stopped his carriage and said to me, 'Get thee in,' and I did. I think you will get to Mr. Lincoln faster through this person. Ask the guards at the Executive Mansion to see that this reaches her tonight. Wait outside. Expect to have her maid come for you."

Truth stared down at the note. It was addressed "To Madam Lincoln from Mr. Frederick Douglass." The president's wife!

"I thank thee, sir," Truth said sincerely.

"Good luck to you, child."

Twenty minutes later, the two black people and Truth stood before a large house with columns and gardens on either side. They were let in through the iron gates by Union soldiers. More armed soldiers stopped them as they approached the entrance, and the address on the note was once more examined. It was now handed to a young soldier, who took it around the side of the building.

They waited, listening to crickets and breathing in the sour smell of the brackish water behind the White House. Just as the moon rose in the early evening sky some fifteen minutes later, a plump, middle-aged black woman wearing a lacy white apron came to them through the front door. She said softly, "For Mr. Douglass's sake, Mrs. Lincoln will see you for a few minutes. Come with me."

They followed the woman, who led them to a

side door that she held open. She said, "Follow me, please."

They walked down corridors that turned this way and that, past rooms with closed doors and others with doors opened wide enough for Truth to peep in and see velvet and satin draperies, lavishly gilded furniture, and pure white lace curtains that made her gasp because they were so beautiful. The maid finally stopped at a door, knocked and listened. Then she stood back to let the three visitors enter.

This room was mostly blue and white, and though it wasn't large, it was furnished with fine pieces—settees, a desk, several chairs, and a large, highly polished rocking chair. A small, plump woman sat in it, reading. Her skin was powdery white, her hair dark, and her eyes dark. Her low-cut gown was white muslin with skirt flounces of deep rose. Red stones circled her neck and dangled from her ears. She set her book down and said in a low voice, "I am Mary Lincoln. Mr. Douglass says a Quaker girl came to ask a favor of him. He has suggested that I help you. What is it you ask, child."

Nudged again by Liley, Truth told her story, finishing with, "I want to ask the president to write a letter for Robert to get him out of prison."

Mrs. Lincoln nodded. "Robert, you say, and Todd? Did you know that I have a son named Robert and that my maiden name is Todd."

"No, ma'am, I didn't."

"I came here from Illinois. You speak like someone from the West."

"I am from Indiana, Mrs. Lincoln. I'm an orphan now, so I live with my mother's folks in North Carolina. I came north with my uncle, but he got hurt in New York City. He's a conductor on the Underground Railroad. He sent my friends here north."

Mrs. Lincoln's dark brows rose. "Well, that is quite a tale. Your cousins refused to take up arms for the Confederacy?"

"That's right." Truth hesitated, but then added, "Or for the North, either. Robert shouldn't be in one of thy prisons then, should he, ma'am?"

Mrs. Lincoln let out her breath. She got up and went to the desk, sat down, and said, "Give me Robert's full name, and yours, too."

Truth replied, "Robert Bardwell, a Friend from North Carolina, and Tabitha Ruth Hopkins."

Mrs. Lincoln wrote quickly. "Wait here," she said. She went through a door that connected her room with another and left the door half open.

A man's husky, weary-sounding voice asked, "What is it, my dear? You know how I feel about interruptions." He gave a deep sigh.

The president! Truth's flesh froze, and she clasped her hands to her mouth in fright. She could hear murmurings but nothing more, until President Lincoln said, "Yes, I see. I see." Then there was a long silence.

From where she stood, Truth peeked through the partially open door. At first, no one was visible. But all at once, she saw against some white curtains the silhouette of a very tall, very thin, stooped man. Truth saw him hand something to Mrs. Lincoln. Truth's heart gave a leap. He'd given her a piece of white paper!

The president said something else that Truth could not make out, and then Mary Lincoln bustled out, shutting the door and handing the folded paper to Truth. With a little smile, she said, "I know that my husband has a fond spot for Quakers. Take this to that prison in New York State. Give it to the warden. But how will you get your cousin home, my dear?"

"On the Underground Railroad—the same way we came up, ma'am."

"You are brave, but then I'm told that most Quakers are. I wish you a safe journey."

"Oh, thank thee. We thank thee," cried Truth. "Thank the president, too."

Mary Lincoln smiled. "I've already thanked him for you. You will see that your name is on the outside of the note."

Liley touched Truth's arm and said, "All of us thank you for your trouble, ma'am. We won't take up more of your time."

Mrs. Lincoln nodded and reached for a tapestry bellpull beside a damask drapery. Her maid came in at once. The president's wife told her, "Show these good people out."

Once more, Truth, Squire, and Liley followed the black woman to the side door, where she spoke to the guards. She walked them to the gates, speaking to every guard, and then left them to go back to the mansion.

When they were alone, Truth read the words "For Tabitha Hopkins, Quaker" and unfolded the piece of paper under a flickering gas street lamp. Written in crooked handwriting, the note read:

Commandant, Elmira Prison:

Release the Quaker prisoner Robert Bardwell from North Carolina to his family, represented by Tabitha Ruth Hopkins. Return this note to the Quaker girl, so no other men can take him prisoner or force him into the Union army.

A. Lincoln

Truth held the note to her chest with both hands. She had what she'd come so far to get! She asked Squire, "What's the fastest way to Elmira?"

"A train. We'll go tonight. We can sleep on it."

"I still have some money. I will give it to thee."

"No, you keep that. You'll have to buy two tickets from Elmira to Maryland." He chuckled. "From there on, it won't cost you anything, but the ride won't be so comfortable."

"I know, but I don't care. Robert won't care, either. We'll be going home!"

Liley said, "He could stay in the North and be safe with that letter. So could you. We'd find you work here."

Truth shook her head. "No. Robert will want to go home. And so do I."

CHAPTER 11

Elmira

Exhausted, Truth didn't pay attention to
the route they took on the railroad that night.
She slept whenever she could during the stifling,
muggy August night. The wind that came into
the open train windows woke her often as it
blew in stinking smoke and sparks from the
ever-puffing locomotive. Shepherded by Squire,
who seemed to need little rest, they changed
trains twice. In the morning, Truth scarcely remembered she'd done that.

By mid-morning, she sat in her seat eating
cold bacon rolls that Squire had bought at the
last depot stop. As she looked out the window
at a dusty green landscape dotted with small

towns, she asked Squire, "Does thee know all the railroad lines?"

Liley answered for him as he smiled and closed his eyes. "The printer he works for prints railroad timetables."

"Oh."

Liley went on, "We have a new last name now, Squire and I. We chose Bardwell. I think you will guess why."

Truth licked her fingers as she said, "My ma was a Bardwell. The Bardwells will be pleased. I'll tell them all about thee and how kind thee have been and how much thee have helped us. I will never forget thee." Suddenly she remembered something. "Mr. Fields, that slave catcher who was after Squire, joined the Confederate army and got hurt real bad. He lost a leg. He won't be hunting anyone anymore."

"No, he won't," agreed Liley. "The North is going to win this war. That'll stop slavery forever."

"I do hope so, and fast." Truth asked Squire, "When will we get to Elmira?"

"Around noon. We'll go straight to the prison."

Truth shuddered. Quakers knew much of

prisons. They had often been jailed in England and America.

Elmira was a neat little town located north and west of New York City, near the Pennsylvania border. The townspeople didn't bother Truth as she, Squire, and Liley got off at the depot. The men and women stared at them for only a moment before going on about their business.

Squire could not hire a horse cab, but a man with a wagon was willing to take them all to the prison. Truth could see he was curious about their errand, but he did not say anything except to ask, "Do you want me to wait outside for you?"

"Yes, we do," answered Truth, feeling President Lincoln's note in her pocket. It gave her courage.

Her first sight of the prison at the foot of a long hill dismayed her. A twelve-foot-high fence of new lumber surrounded it. Guards dressed in blue walked its length with rifles on their shoulders.

The driver took the wagon to the gates and drew it to a halt. Truth looked past the gates to long rows of one-story wooden buildings and rows and rows of white tents.

Two armed soldiers at the gate came forward with another soldier, who asked them sharply, "What is your business here?"

Squire answered, "To see the commandant. The girl here has a paper from the president."

The man said sternly, "Let me see that, miss."

Truth surrendered the note. The soldier read it quickly and said only, "Yes?"

She asked, "Does thee know Robert Bardwell of North Carolina? Is he here?"

"There are some eight thousand Confederate prisoners of war here. No, I don't know the name." He turned to the other soldier. "Open the gates. Let this girl through. I'll take her to the commandant's office. The rest of you wait here outside."

Liley hugged Truth and whispered, "Go on, child. Good luck to you. We'll wait by the wagon."

Truth nodded. As she went through the gates, she asked the soldier, "Please, sir, give me my note from President Lincoln. It is mine. He wrote that it was."

The man looked at her but didn't give her

back the paper. He led the way toward an un-painted wooden building where the U.S. flag hung limp in the warm air. A foul odor drifted to Truth's nostrils. It was so evil, she put her finger under her nose.

The soldier grinned. "That'd be our famous Foster's Pond you're getting a whiff of. It's rotten, but good enough for the Rebels here."

He took her up onto the porch, opened the door, and brought her into an office that was furnished only with a desk, some chairs, and a rack of guns. He said to a young soldier behind the desk, "This girl wants to see the commandant. She's got a letter for him." Now he gave Truth the note.

"A girl?" The soldier stood up. "Say, I see she's a Quaker. Where did she come from?"

"Indiana," said Truth. "I've come about my cousin, Robert Bardwell. He's a prisoner here, and I want to see him. I have a note from Abraham Lincoln that says I can."

The first soldier said, "She's a bold piece, this one."

"A letter from the president, you say?"

Truth gave it to the second man, who read it, looked hard at her, and said, "I'll take you to the commandant. Wait here."

The young northerner went inside a door at the rear of the front office and closed it after himself. But he was back at once. "Come in. The commandant will see you."

The commandant, who sat in another bare room, was a big soldier with gray side-whiskers, a red face, and sharp dark eyes. President Lincoln's letter was on the table in front of him. "Sit down, girl," he ordered. "Tell me how you got this."

Truth said, "I am Tabitha Ruth Hopkins from Indiana. I moved to North Carolina when my father died. Robert Bardwell is my North Carolina cousin. We are Friends. He was forced into the Confederate army. That was not fair. The Union army captured him and brought him here. I came up from North Carolina to get him."

"How in the dickens did you get here?" The man's bristly gray eyebrows rose.

"On the Underground Railroad. I went to see President Lincoln. Mr. Frederick Douglass helped me, too. The president wrote me that note. It's real."

"Well, this beats all! Yes, I believe it is real. This paper's from the Executive Mansion. It says so. And that is Lincoln's signature. I've seen it before." The officer got up and went to the filthy, flyblown window. "I guess I'll have to release your cousin to you by order of the president. I'll have him brought here now."

Truth felt the tension drain out of her. She'd done it! In the deep recesses of her bonnet, she smiled. Suddenly, an idea struck her. She knew it would sound strange to the officer, but she blurted out all the same, "Please, sir, tell him his kettle cousin has come for him."

"Kettle cousin, eh? A poor relation, are you?"

"Yes, sir, an orphan."

"Sit over there on the bench. I'll check the records on him and send a soldier to find him." The commandant left the room and closed the door after himself.

Truth went over to the bench and sat down. She waited and waited, swinging her feet. Finally, she heard the outer door open and the baritone hum of men's voices. Then the second door was flung open.

There in the doorway, between two armed soldiers, stood a gaunt, sallow-faced young man with a black beard and long, uncombed dark hair. His shirt and trousers were dirty, and his shoes were old and patched.

He gazed dully at Truth, who now took off

her bonnet. Finally, he exclaimed, "It *is* thee, Truth! That is my mother's dress. How did thee . . . ?"

Truth was so overcome by the sight of her cousin's tattered appearance that she could only stammer, "I . . . I . . ."

The commandant broke in, "Oh, she will find words to tell you later on. She doesn't lack for them. I must release you to her. Go, Robert Bardwell. You are a free man."

"Free? How is that?"

"Mr. Lincoln has decreed it."

"The president?"

"Yes, Bardwell, the president." The commandant was now at his desk writing. As Robert looked in disbelief at Truth, the officer gave her Lincoln's note and his own scrawled authorization to surrender Quaker prisoner Robert Bardwell to her.

When she had received both papers, Truth put on her bonnet and took her cousin's arm. She thanked the grim commandant and led Robert out of the office. She couldn't help but notice that the arm she held was skin and bone. He was so thin! As they slowly walked down the hall, she asked him, "Is thee wounded, Robert?"

"No," he said wearily, "but I have malaria and I will need quinine. That's what they gave me here sometimes."

"We shall get thee well. We got Todd well."

Robert stopped. "Thee has Todd at home?" he asked, amazed.

"Yes, he is hiding at the Rocks. Robert, thee can stay here in the North as a free man if thee wants. Or thee can come home with me. What does thee choose?"

"Home," he breathed softly.

"I had guessed that."

As they left the prison and the gates were shut behind them, Truth suddenly heard a shout from the sentry's walk. Looking up, she saw the commandant standing there. All at once, he shook his head as if in disbelief, then snapped off a salute and smiled. Impulsively, Truth took off her bonnet again and swung it by its strings in a wave. She and Squire helped Robert into the wagon, and they started back to Elmira.

As they rode, Truth told him bits and pieces of the events leading up to his rescue—but not about Matthew Bardwell. That could be told later, she decided.

In Elmira, the driver waited while Truth bought Robert a jacket and straw hat at the general store and some quinine from the pharmacist. At long last, she and her cousin were in the depot, waiting for the train that would take them away from Elmira forever.

Sitting beside Robert, Truth sighed. How weary she was of the click-clack of train wheels. The trip ahead on the other "railroad" would be far worse, however. Truth looked at Robert and wondered, would he be strong enough for that journey? The hiding would be hard on him. How she wished Uncle Matthew was there to help her take his son home! But he lay in a sick bed himself, so it was up to her.

Squire and Liley's New York City–bound train came first. They got up, took their carpetbags, and then turned to Robert and Truth. Liley wept and embraced them warmly. As Squire shook hands with them, Truth noticed that he had tears in his eyes.

"How can we ever thank thee?" Robert asked him brokenly.

"You don't have to. You helped us, now we help you. When we get to Liberia and the war's over, we'll write to you."

Liley added, "If the baby we're expecting is a boy, we'll name him Matthew Robert Todd; if it's a girl, Tabitha Ruth."

"Call her just Truth, please," corrected a flattered Truth.

"Good-bye, my friend." Liley kissed her on the cheek and boarded the train.

Squire said from the platform, "I'll send a telegraph message to Friend Quisenbery as soon as we arrive in New York City. He'll expect you. We'll see Matthew Bardwell right away, too. We'll tell him the good news about Robert."

"See my pa? Where is he?" asked Robert, quizzically.

As the train puffed out with the former slaves aboard, Truth now told her cousin the rest of her story. She said gently, "Thy father is in New York City. He is sick. But he is being well looked after by a Quaker doctor. He came north with me, and a mob attacked him because he is a Quaker. When he is better, Friends will send him home."

Robert sat quietly as she spoke. Finally, he roused himself and, sounding amazed, said, "Then thee will be our guide?"

"Yes." Truth managed to laugh. "I remember the way." More somberly, she added, "I don't think I will ever forget it."

CHAPTER 12

Going Home

EXHAUSTED, ROBERT SLEPT much of the way to Maryland, awakening only to change trains and eat the beef sandwiches Truth bought for them at the depots.

Friend Quisenbery met them at the Hagerstown depot that evening. Smiling, he said, "I got a telegram. Thee has performed a miracle, child. I take it this is Robert." Then, looking about, he added, "But where is thy uncle?"

Truth answered, "Hurt in New York. I'll tell thee on the way to thy house." Turning to Robert, she said quietly, "Thee and I will be in Virginia by morning. Rest now. Kind people risk their lives to help us."

151

"I know," he replied, "and I am truly thankful."

The Quisenberys fed them and let them sleep a few hours. All too soon, the weary travelers were blindfolded and led outside. Truth gripped the two Quisenberys' hands in turn, thanking them and receiving their blessings. Then she and Robert were on their way over the border in the creaking, jolting buggy.

That evening, the two cousins rode in the hearse to the house with children and the secret room. As before, Truth saw no one but was fed courteously and given a soft bed.

At their next stop, the old man Truth recognized from his grating voice came for them in his wagon, and they spent the following day in his root cellar among his turnips, potatoes, and cabbages.

By this time, Robert's malaria had returned, and his teeth were chattering. Truth gave him some quinine, and, to comfort him, she said, "It will please thee to know that our own Friend Buchan will be here tonight. He will put us in the false bottom of his wagon."

"Friend Buchan?" asked the shivering Robert.

"Yes, and Martha. She may come, too. She has worried over thee and prayed for thee all along."

Robert's voice was strong as he replied, "Then we're almost home—almost home!"

Truth and Robert lay in the false bottom of the Buchans' wagon as the Quaker, with Martha beside him, drove up to the front of the Bardwell house. Robert was quite ill, sicker than he had been since they left Elmira. He shuddered with chills and then blazed with fever. He had been hidden by day in the harness room at the Buchans' farm, covered with blankets. Sister Buchan and Martha had tried to get him to eat, but he had taken only water.

As they had set out, Robert had raved in a fitful sleep and tossed about. They had to go on, though. The Rocks were a far safer place to hide than the farm.

After dark, Robert had been half carried to the wagon and loaded inside. Truth crawled in and lay beside him. She had a towel to put over his mouth to stop him from crying out.

When the Buchans' wagon finally stopped moving and the wagon bottom was opened, Truth knew that she and Robert were home at last. As Friend Buchan and Martha helped her out, she could see Aunt Elizabeth and Lucy standing there with their lanterns, a look of joy on their faces.

As soon as their neighbors helped Robert out, Truth's aunt set the lantern down and pulled him into her embrace. "Robert? Is it really thee?" she cried. Then she asked in terror, "Why is thee so hot? And where is thy father?"

Truth answered her quickly, to put an end to her worst fear. "He is in New York City. At the house of a Quaker doctor."

"Is he sick, too?"

"Yes, but the doctor and Squire are seeing to his welfare."

"Squire, the slave who came here?"

"Yes, he and his wife helped me in the North." As the Bardwell women helped Robert into the house, Truth told of her journey one more time.

When she finished, her aunt said in amazement, "Thee did that alone, child?"

"No, as I told thee, Squire and Liley helped me. Aunt, Robert has malaria." Truth took the bottle of quinine powder from her pocket. "You must give this to him. Brew it in a tea. He needs it now." Suddenly, Truth's voice faltered.

"Oh, Aunt Elizabeth, I don't feel well. I feel so weak."

"Martha," called William Buchan, who was helping to hold Robert on his feet. "Take Truth up to her bed."

"Yes, Father."

Truth felt her friend's arm go around her waist. Then she was pulled through the house and up the stairs to her room. Still dressed, she fell onto the bed. As Martha unlaced her boots and took them off, she told Truth, "Go to sleep. Thee has earned it. Todd and Father will get Robert to the Rocks and hide him."

Truth slept for a long time. When she awoke, she washed at the basin and changed into clean clothes. Not until breakfast did she talk with her aunt, who was waiting for her at the kitchen table. She told Truth that Robert was conscious and had had a joyful reunion with Todd. He was, however, worried about his father, as was she.

Truth shared their concern. She told her aunt, "Dr. Porter will send news, I'm sure."

The woman nodded agreement and said, "Last meeting day the elders and I talked. They mentioned thee. They think highly of thee. I

155

have sent a message to them, and they will know thee has returned with Robert." Aunt Elizabeth smiled. "Thee is a true daughter to us—a blessing. Did thee see that good man, Mr. Lincoln?"

"No, only his shadow."

"Oh, that is a pity."

"He wrote this letter for me." Now Truth handed the note to her aunt.

The woman's eyes filled with tears as she read and returned it. "It is a pity no one can be told of what thee has done."

Truth replied, "After the war, it can be related. Then thee can frame this letter and put it on the wall to keep forever."

The girl ate some molasses-soaked corn bread kept ready for her. When she was finished, her aunt turned the conversation to Matthew Bardwell. "Oh, Truth, I hope he's getting better. You say they hit him on his head?"

"Yes."

"Injuries to the head can take time to heal." The woman's face was pale and anxious. "We must have patience and hope for the best. At least, we can be thankful that Todd and Robert are safe. And, Truth, I have some happy news to tell thee." Aunt Elizabeth now smiled, wiped

156

her eyes with her apron, and said, "There'll be another one of us come spring. Lucy is having a baby—to be born in March."

All the time that Truth spoke with the grave-faced elders outside the meetinghouse at the next First Day meeting, she was aware of Lydia's watchful astonishment. Talking quickly, she told them all that had happened since she and her uncle had left the Bardwell farm. They listened silently, and finally one of the men said, "Thee did well, child. This will be a star in thy crown. Go now—the girl over there waits for thee."

Truth now ran to Lydia, who asked, "Why did the elders speak with thee, Truth?"

Truth was ready for the question and said, "My uncle hurt himself in Goldsboro and is still at the doctor's house there. They were asking after his condition."

Oh, if she could only tell Lydia everything, too, but she could not! Instead she said, "Has thee heard from Mr. Hartling recently?"

"No, but he should write to thee, too, not just to us." Lydia giggled. "He should have asked thy uncle's permission to write thee, but he had no time. It's thee he fancies. I think he would become a Friend for thy sake."

"Oh, Lydia!" scolded Truth, whose cheeks became pinker as her friend spoke.

Lydia just giggled again.

CHAPTER 13

A Dreadful Surprise at Bentonville

WHILE TRUTH AND Martha went on with Michael Hartling's work, Robert gained health slowly. Todd still chafed as a prisoner who could come out only after dark. The corn, harvested in the early fall by Quaker Friends, was shucked and put in the corncrib for storage.

They had received news from the North about Matthew Bardwell by way of the Underground Railroad. He was better, but his head had been fractured. He still suffered from headaches and dizziness and was not able to travel.

In late September they learned that a Union general named Sherman had taken Atlanta, Georgia, and was continuing on a march

159

through that state to the sea in hopes of subduing it totally.

Winter came with only one piece of news—Abraham Lincoln had been reelected.

Through it all, the Bardwells went on with their lives—Truth teaching and Aunt Elizabeth doing what she could with shortages of food and everything else. The hams they had salted down had been taken by confiscating Confederate soldiers, and their corncrib had been plundered. They were left with one sorry horse.

Early in February, Friend Buchan came one night to tell them, "This Union general Sherman went across Georgia to Savannah on the sea. Now he is marching north through South Carolina. If he takes South Carolina, the war could be over."

"Hurray!" shouted Truth.

William Buchan nodded. "Yes, but there's a rub. There are Confederate soldiers aplenty in Goldsboro and others in South Carolina. If they can get together to stop Sherman, they'll try to do it."

"How?" asked Truth.

"Oh, they'll fight," said Robert quietly.

"They're a courageous lot. It'll be a last-stand fight, too."

"Where will they fight?" asked his mother.

Robert said gravely, "Wherever the two armies come across each other—that's how battles happen." He sighed. "I know. I saw some of those battles, right out in front. I'll never forget the sound of the drums and the bugles behind me! The army uses them to drive the men on."

"Oh, what good comes out of this?" asked Elizabeth Bardwell, her hands on the sides of her head.

"An end to slavery, Ma," Todd replied.

Another Quaker, Lucy's father, came riding through a rainstorm in mid-March. By the smile on his broad pink face, he brought good news. As he dismounted, stepping down into a puddle, he told Elizabeth Bardwell and Truth, "Lucy's had her child. It is a girl born last night near midnight."

"Oh, what wonderful news," cried Truth's aunt. "Todd will be so pleased. He's so worried. He wanted to be with Lucy."

Now the man frowned. "There's more news. The talk from Goldsboro is that Yankee armies are in North Carolina. There's no danger right now as I see it." He nodded at Truth. "Lucy asked me to bring thee back with me when I go, Truth. My wife's ailing, and thee can help her. Can thee leave thy school?"

"Yes," Truth answered. "Martha Buchan can teach. There are few children now."

"Good—get thee ready to stay a week. My horse can carry double. I hid hay for her this winter. She has fared well."

While Lucas Coxey went to the Rocks to speak with Todd, Truth ran to her room. She put nightgowns and warm clothing into a bundle and was ready when he returned.

An hour later, clasping the man's broad back as she perched behind him, the two of them reached the Goldsboro road that ran east and west. Here Friend Coxey halted. "Truth, someone is coming, riding fast."

Truth listened. Sure enough, there was a pounding, and down behind a tree-lined bend came a rider in Confederate gray. He flashed past, splashing them and shouting, "Get off this road! Go home." Then he was gone.

"What does it mean?" Truth asked Lucy's father.

"He was a courier, I think. The way he was

riding, he's on urgent business. Let us take his advice. It was well meant." Lucy's father turned the sorrel mare onto a side road and nudged her into a canter.

Some time later, Lucas Coxey suddenly reined in at the top of a hill. Hidden behind his back, Truth could not see why. She asked, "What is it? Is there a swamp below?"

"No." The man's voice was hollow. "It's cavalry—Union and Confederate. They're fighting. Listen."

While she craned her neck to see below, Truth listened. What she heard were the shouts of men, the neighing of horses, and the ringing clang of metal on metal as the soldiers' sabers came slashing down. Though they were far away, she could see them as gray and blue figures mounted on horses, all struggling in a cluster. Sometimes a riderless horse darted out of the battle, leaving a man behind on the earth.

She moaned, "Oh, Friend Coxey! What can we do?"

"Turn around and take another road. We can't go down to that. Thee should not have seen it!"

As he reined the mare about, Truth buried her head in his back. Men were bleeding and dying down there. They rode to the foot of the hill and down a narrow path that could scarcely be called a road. They were on it only a little time before Coxey reined in again.

A Union officer accompanied by six troopers was across the little road. The big-bearded man was dirty but had on a gold-braided uniform. He demanded, "Who'd you be? Do you live around here? By your hat, I see you're an accursed Quaker who lets better men do his fighting for him."

Lucy's father kept his dignity. "I am Friend Lucas Coxey. I live near Bentonville. Who would thee be?"

"My name is no matter to you. Who is that girl with you? Is she a slave? I can't see her face or her hands. If she is, let her go free or it will not go well with you. All blacks are to be free."

Truth hastily removed her big bonnet and a mitten so she could be seen.

The officer grunted. "I see. There's to be fighting here most likely. Take your family and get them west of here where they'll be safest."

"And if we do not go?"

"Then whatever happens is your own fault for being fools." The officer shrugged. He raised his right hand, reined his gray past Coxey's mare, and was followed at a trot by his men in single file.

"A battle?" Truth repeated quietly as she put her bonnet on again.

"So it appears."

They met no more soldiers on the way, and in an hour's time they reached the Coxey's two-story house. A small, thin, shawl-covered woman came running to them from the front doorway, waving her apron.

"Who is that?" asked Truth, who had never seen her before.

"The midwife from Goldsboro. Nancy Andrews is her name. She's been free for years. She bought her way out of slavery and bought her husband out, too. He's a carpenter. She's to stay here for a day or two more."

The black woman touched Lucas Coxey's stirrup and cried, "There have been soldiers here, Confederate ones. They told us to leave 'cause they might fight here. We can't—Mrs. Coxey or Mrs. Bardwell or the baby—not yet we can't."

"I know that, Nancy. We'll stay and take our chances."

Truth slid down and asked, "Please take me to see Lucy and the baby."

The baby lay yawning in the curve of Lucy's arm. She was tiny, wrinkled, and red, with tufts of dark hair the color of Todd's. The new mother told Truth, "She's to be called Elizabeth Mary, after Todd's mother and mine."

"Thee has chosen a good, strong name."

Just before noon on the next day, a sudden enormous booming sound made Truth and Lucy start, and the baby open her eyes. "What is it?" asked Lucy.

Lucas Coxey came into the bedroom, with Nancy behind him. "That was a cannon. I've heard cannons fired on the Fourth of July. Lucy, I believe we must move thee down from this floor. Nancy, take the baby and I'll carry Lucy. Truth, bring the bedding and anything else Nancy tells thee we'll be needing. We may see a battle. God be with us!"

CHAPTER 14

A Battle—and Peace

Lucas Coxey was right. The battle began and raged around them for three long, windy, rain-swept days. For the rest of her life, Truth Hopkins would remember the horrible noises that made her shriek and clap her hands over her ears as she lay flat on the parlor floor beside Nancy and the Coxeys.

On the first day of the fighting, a whistling cannonball crashed through the house, and a second one shattered the stairs an hour later. They dared not raise their heads to look out the windows, though they could hear men screaming and shouting hoarsely as they attacked. Gunfire raked the house but did not penetrate its heavy wooden sides. When attacks came, there was a constant thudding of cannon fire. Gunpowder smoke floated through the broken windows, stifling, sickening them.

Afraid to stand, they crawled into the kitchen for dry corn bread and pails of bad-tasting water that had been used for rinsing the laundry. Truth thought she would go mad with terror as she prayed over and over for the battle to end. Was God deaf?

Beside her, Nancy prayed, too. Lucy's mother sobbed for hours in her husband's arms. Lucy wept, too. Only the baby seemed undisturbed, nursing, fussing, and falling asleep.

For Truth, the worst of all was the bugling— not the drums or the thunder of cannons or the thud of hooves. She'd learned from Todd and Robert that bugles meant an attack on foot. Bugles meant that men on foot, led by drummers, marched in rows toward other advancing men. When they met, they shot at one another at point-blank range. After the bugles, there always came the howls and shrieks of pain as the soldiers then clashed hand to hand with rifle butts and bayonets. To think that Robert had been in the middle of such horrors time and time again! It was a wonder to Truth that she had not found a madman at Elmira.

Thinking of him made the girl crawl over to retch into the corner hole Lucas Coxey had dug into the floorboards with his knife to serve as a privy. By the end of the second day, her stomach ached from vomiting. She hurt all over from the cold and dampness, the hardness of the bare floors, and the sleeplessness. Would they die, all of them, if the house caught fire? Robert had said that forests could burn in battles, so why not houses?

At long last, the clamor of battle ceased. Deep voices were heard on what was left of the Coxey porch. One said, "Wonder if there's anybody inside. Anybody alive, I mean." It was a northern voice, not a southern one.

Lucas Coxey shouted, "Yes, we're in here. We're all alive. Who are thee? Can we come out now?"

"We're a detail from the Union army, Johnny Reb, and we've come to pick up our dead."

Friend Coxey cried, "We aren't Rebels. We're Quakers."

"Oh," said a second voice, without enthusiasm. "Well, come on out, but it ain't a pretty sight. There's dead all around. We won't shoot you. General Sherman has moved on, chasing down Rebs only he knows where. We're left behind to clean up the dirty work."

Truth crept to the nearest window and looked out onto an ocean of mud, where blue-coats walked about from man to fallen man. Once identified, the dead men were hauled by their arms or legs to wagons and tossed inside. Gray-coated soldiers hunted, too, bending, turning over bodies and dragging them to wagons. The girl shuddered and closed her eyes. How horrible war was! When she had arrived at the Coxeys', there had been grass, a white fence, and shade trees. There was nothing now but mud and stumps.

A small Union corporal opened the door and came into the house. He took off his hat and scratched his head, his red hair shining in the sunshine. "Hey, look at all the folks on the floor—and a baby, too. Well, we won't be here too long. Then you can set things to right."

Truth said, "Could I go home now?"

The man stopped, stiffening. "You don't talk like a Reb. Are you?"

"No, I was born in Indiana. I live near Goldsboro now. I don't live here in Bentonville."

He nodded. "If I was a little gal alone like you, I wouldn't head out anywhere. Stay here a spell."

Lucy's mother told her weakly, "He's right, Truth. Stay."

The soldier pointed at Nancy. "Is she a slave?"

"No." Nancy Andrews stood up. "I'm free, and I've been free for fifteen years. I get paid for what I do."

"Glad to hear it," the Yankee said, and left, shutting the door.

Five days went by. Truth and Nancy were now able to use the stove, cooking what they could find. Lucas Coxey boarded up parts of the house. The soldiers didn't come near them again, though one night some skinned rabbits appeared on the back porch, a gift from some unknown soldier.

On the sixth day, a heavyset black man drove up in a mule-drawn wagon. "Hamp!" cried Nancy, who hastily handed the just-bathed baby to Truth and ran out the front door. "Hamp, Hamp! It's me, Nancy."

"Who's that?" Truth asked Lucy.

"Her husband. He's probably come to fetch her home."

"Could I go back with them?" asked the girl.

"Ask them. Pa and I can manage here now. Nancy says she'll send a woman friend from town to help us, and Ma is getting better."

Hamp Andrews remained for a few days at the Coxeys', surveying the damage to the house and helping to repair it. As he was leaving for supplies one morning, Truth asked him, "Are the roads safe?"

"I reckon they are. I saw only two soldiers on the way, and both of them were on foot and wounded. There're Yankees in Goldsboro, and I think they did what they wanted to do when they won their battle here." Then Hamp grinned. "This here's the end of March. Folks say the war's just about all over and done with, and there'll be peace pretty soon. Come on, Quaker girl, climb on up inside my wagon and find you a place to sit. I'll take you home right now."

With a whoop of joy, Truth ran to gather up her things and say good-bye to Lucy and the baby. Just before she clambered into the wagon, Friend Coxey came to her, put his hands on her shoulders, and said, "We thank thee, Truth Hopkins. When I asked thee to come here with me, I did not expect to bring thee to a battle-field. Thee is a brave girl and a credit to the Bardwells. I will rebuild here, and plant elms and fruit trees again as soon as I can. We hope and pray there was no fighting at the Bardwell farm."

"So do I. So do I. It's what I kept thinking of till it hurt my head." Truth buried her head against the man's shoulder for a tearful moment before she climbed into the wagon where Hamp waited for her.

A few hours later, Truth was home, and, thank goodness, the Bardwell place was the same. After bidding farewell to Hamp, she ran to the house, flung open the front door, and yelled, "Aunt, I'm home!"

No, she was wrong! Something had happened here, too. The parlor was stripped of all its furnishings. It was as bare as could be—just white-washed walls and a now-muddy floor.

"Aunt Elizabeth!" she screamed.

"Truth!" came a shout behind her, and her aunt came around from the back of the house. She cried, "Thank goodness you're here. We heard there was fighting near Bentonville."

"I was in it! Lucy and the baby are all right. What happened here?"

"Yankees came. They took whatever they had a fancy to and ate all they could find.

"The soldiers searched the place but never found the cave in the rocks. They're all right. Nobody hurt me, either."

"Oh, Aunt Elizabeth." Truth flung her arms around the woman's neck, and they both wept. When they were calmer, Truth told her, "In Goldsboro, people say the war's almost over. The North will surely win."

"Oh, let that be true."

Truth shivered, remembering the terrible days of fighting, and muttered, "Let me never hear a bugle again."

In the cave that evening, Todd, Robert, and their mother listened closely to Truth's account of what had gone on at Bentonville. They nodded but said little.

Suddenly, Todd said, "You say the baby looks like me."

"I'd say so. Elizabeth Mary stood the battle better than anyone else."

All three Bardwells laughed when they heard that. It was their first laugh in a long time.

* * *

174

Truth and Martha did not resume teaching school when Truth returned from the Coxeys. Boys and girls who would have gone were kept at home to help with the spring planting and farmyard chores. Truth and her aunt did the plowing and then dropped in the corn kernels and sowed the grain they'd hidden under the hearthstone with their own store of dry food. No one, Rebel or Yankee, had ever found this hiding place.

On a dark Monday night, Friend Buchan brought his wagon to the Bardwell farm. He didn't come alone. Martha was with him—and someone else too. Matthew Bardwell was sitting on the wagon seat beside her!

When his wife saw him, she whispered to Truth, "Go fetch Robert and Todd. Quickly!"

Never had Truth run so fast. Her cousins followed closely behind her. They lifted their father down and stood in a knot of family, embracing him. Truth stood to the side.

She heard her aunt ask tearfully, "Are thee well, Matthew?"

"Well enough, wife. I do not see so well out of one eye now, but I am well enough to keep our farm."

"Thee came ahead of the news of thy arrival,

husband. It must have been because there was fighting here."

"Yes," agreed William Buchan. "He came to us as a surprise."

"Who cares how I came?" said Uncle Matthew. "I am here and I shall stay. They claim the war will be ended very soon." Now he turned to Truth and beckoned her. "Come here and join us, daughter. Thee, too, is one of the Bardwell family. Thee has done a great deal for us, it seems to me. Friend Buchan says thee brought Robert home all by thyself."

"Not really. Squire and Liley helped me. Did they go to Liberia, Uncle Matthew?"

"Yes, they went. They came to tell me farewell."

"Come into the house and rest, Matthew," said Elizabeth Bardwell. "I have a little tea hidden. I kept it for thee to drink upon thy return. There's fresh-baked corn bread and plum jam."

After hitching the horse and wagon to the gate, the Buchans, too, came inside for a while. Truth noted how Robert glanced again and again at a blooming Martha. She smiled as she told herself, he takes notice of her now!

* * *

Finally, the war ended. A passing rider brought the joyous news in April. Truth heard it at the front gate and ran to tell the Bardwells, first her uncle and aunt, then Todd and Robert. Her cousins left the Rocks at once, walking freely into the bright April sunshine. A half hour later, Todd saddled the thin old bay and headed out for Bentonville to see Lucy and the baby.

First Day came four days later. For the first time in four years, all of the Bardwells went to meeting together. How the Friends stared as they arrived in a neighbor's borrowed wagon— stared and then smiled. Outside, the elders came up to speak with Truth before the meeting. One by one they touched her bonnet or arm as they left her. She felt so very strange, not weak but strong. Everything around her had suddenly become so bright, so clear—each new leaf on the trees, each gleaming blade of grass. Everything now shone golden.

Truth felt her blood course through her veins, and her steps seemed more buoyant as she started for the meetinghouse door. It was as if she floated there.

As she passed by Lydia, her friend pulled a

ragged envelope from her pocket and waved it at her. Truth smiled. Yes, that was fitting today, a letter from Mr. Hartling.

She took her seat and fell silent, but the strange feeling didn't leave her. It continued to grow, filling her. She waited. Then she saw one of the elders nod and the old woman beside him smile slightly.

Tabitha Ruth Hopkins rose. Standing, she said in a clear, low voice, "I am too young to speak to thee, I know, but there is something the Lord has done with me as his poor servant. As the instrument of his grace, I feel the need to share my experience with all of thee. . . ."

Author's Note

THE QUAKERS

The Society of Friends, an important religious group even today, was founded in England in 1652 by George Fox. Soon known as Quakers (tremblers in the presence of the Holy Spirit), they refused traditional forms of worship used in British churches, such as sermons and choirs. They were pacifists and refused to take oaths. Their beliefs led to their persecution and imprisonment in England.

In 1681, Quaker convert William Penn was

granted Pennsylvania as a royal colony. He viewed it as a refuge for Quakers and other persecuted groups.

The Society flourished in the New World, though its members were persecuted in the United States as well. Their meetinghouses were to be seen up and down the East Coast. Members adopted plain dark garments without buttons or ornamentation and wore special wide-brimmed hats and deep bonnets. By the mid-nineteenth century, there were three groups: the Orthodox Quakers, Hicksites, and Wilburites. Quakers were humanitarians. They believed they answered to a higher law than human laws. God's "Light" could be found in Indians and blacks as well as white men.

Many Quakers were active in the antislavery movement and were involved in operating the Underground Railroad. One prominent figure of the railroad was a North Carolina–born Quaker, Levi Coffin. He operated one of the most successful stations in the entire network. Famous Quakers of this period were poet John Greenleaf Whittier and suffragist Lucretia Mott.

At a time when women were not permitted to

speak in church, Quaker women were encouraged to "testify" on First Day, or Sunday. They were as renowned for their quiet courage and steadfastness as the men. The justification for their taking part in church matters was the New Testament, in which it is written, "Women spoke to Jesus."

Quaker men could serve as soldiers if they chose, but few did. In the Civil War era, many fled to the West or attempted to escape to Canada, but some were caught and forced into the army or arrested and put in military prisons, both Union and Confederate, for refusing to take up arms. The situation was generally worse in the South. The men would usually refuse all military training and fall to the ground when the soldiers advanced on foot firing at one another. What happened to the fictional Bardwells could easily have happened. Men who had fled the Confederate army were concealed in places throughout the South.

Nineteenth-century Quakers used "thee" and "thy" (but not "thou") in addressing members of their faith and nonmembers. The practice died out fairly recently, but I am told that some older Friends still use this mode of address when speaking to one another.

THE UNDERGROUND
RAILROAD

One of the most exciting and secretive parts of United States history revolves around the railroad with no rails, which was used to carry slaves to freedom in the North and in Canada. The people who operated the Underground Railroad in the South were nicknamed "conductors." A conductor knew only the location of the next station and who brought him or her the slaves. Many women and children were involved. Slaves going in only one direction were not blindfolded, but anyone who went and then returned probably would have been, to protect the identities of the conductors. This railroad existed not only in the East but also in the Midwest.

NORTH CAROLINA

North Carolina seceded from the Union in May 1861. However, there was not a great deal of fighting within its borders. In March 1865, the battle of Bentonville, a Union victory, was the last major fight there. It is a historical fact that a family remained in their home through the battle, and survived! North Carolina sent 125,000 men to the Confederacy and lost 40,000 to battle deaths and disease.

PEOPLE IN THE BOOK

Frederick Douglass, who was born a slave in the South around 1817, escaped to the North in 1838, got an education, and became a noted abolitionist orator. His friends in England helped buy him his freedom in 1847. He knew Abraham Lincoln and tried to convince him to enlist black soldiers before Lincoln was ready to do so. That refusal caused a coldness between them for a time. Quakers had befriended the young Douglass as a terrified runaway, so I believe it would have been in his character to favor them. In his later years, he was appointed minister to Haiti.

Mary Todd Lincoln is one of the more controversial figures of the Civil War era. She was considered a vain, somewhat silly woman, and at times was a trial to her husband. Their oldest son, Robert, was her favorite. Her impulsiveness was well known. It would have been like her to intercede for Truth with her husband. After Lincoln's death, she sent Frederick Douglass her husband's walking cane as a memento. She never recovered from her husband's assassination. In 1876, Robert Lincoln committed her to a mental institution. Her last years were spent at her sister's home in Springfield, Illinois.

In 1864, Abraham Lincoln was in failing physical health because of the enormous burden he carried as president. People remarked on his pallor, gauntness, weariness, and cold handshakes. It is historical fact that he favored the Society of Friends. He was known to have said, "If a man is a Friend, he is no prisoner of war." At the time of his assassination in April 1865, an article by a Quaker was found in his pocket. He truly had the power as president to set a prisoner free, and did so.

PLACES IN THE BOOK

I have described Goldsboro, North Carolina; New York City; Washington, D.C.; and Elmira,

New York, as historical accounts have them at the time. Any buildings from the old prison in Elmira have long ago been razed. Trains could be ridden to all four cities, though nineteenth-century train travel could never be considered comfortable, and travel during Civil War days was even less so. Matthew Bardwell and Truth Hopkins would have needed special passes to travel in the South—and dared not request them. Hence, their use of the Underground Railroad.

One of my chief sources in writing this novel was an old and probably rare book entitled *Southern Heroes*, written by Fernando Gale Cartland (Riverside Press, 1895; reprinted by Garland, 1972). When I casually plucked it from a university library shelf, I expected to find brief biographies of southern leaders such as Lee, Stuart, Hood, and Davis. Instead, it was about Quakers in the southern states. This fascinating volume was the genesis of my book.

My research was aided by a number of people: Ramona Dunkley and Carolyn Griffin of the Goldsboro Public Library in North Carolina; Lynn Teft of the Steele Memorial Library in Elmira, New York; and Mary Ellen Chijioke, curator of Friends Historical Library of Swarth-more College in Swarthmore, Pennsylvania, who also provided an informative letter on Quaker speech of the last century.